Her Rancher Bodyguard

Brenda Minton

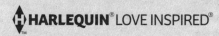

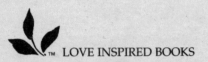

Recycling programs
for this product may
not exist in your area.

LOVE INSPIRED BOOKS

ISBN-13: 978-0-373-81912-6

Her Rancher Bodyguard

www.Harlequin.com

Printed in U.S.A.

She hadn't expected this.

Boone should be in the background, quietly observing. And yet here she sat with her bodyguard and his family, talking of cattle and fixing fences.

A hand settled on her back. She glanced at the man next to her; his dark eyes crinkled at the corners and his mouth quirked, revealing a dimple in his left cheek.

He opened his mouth as if to say something, but a heavy knock on the front door interrupted. He pushed away from the table.

"I think I'll get that." His gaze landed on Kayla. "You stay right where you are until I say otherwise."

"They wouldn't come here," she said.

"We don't know what *they* would or wouldn't do, because we don't know who *they* are. Stay." He walked away.

Kayla avoided looking at the people who still remained at the table. She knew they were looking at her. She knew that her life had invaded theirs.

And she knew that her bodyguard might seem like a relaxed cowboy, but he wasn't. He was the man standing between her and the unknown.

Brenda Minton lives in the Ozarks with her husband, children, cats, dogs and strays. She is a pastor's wife, Sunday school teacher, coffee addict and sleep-deprived. Not in that order. Her dream to be an author for Harlequin started somewhere in the pages of a romance novel about a young American woman stranded in a Spanish castle. Her dreams came true, and twenty-plus books later, she is an author hoping to inspire young girls to dream.

Books by Brenda Minton

Love Inspired

Martin's Crossing

A Rancher for Christmas
The Rancher Takes a Bride
The Rancher's Second Chance
The Rancher's First Love
Her Rancher Bodyguard

Lone Star Cowboy League

A Reunion for the Rancher

Cooper Creek

Christmas Gifts
"Her Christmas Cowboy"
The Cowboy's Holiday Blessing
The Bull Rider's Baby
The Rancher's Secret Wife
The Cowboy's Healing Ways
The Cowboy Lawman
The Cowboy's Christmas Courtship
The Cowboy's Reunited Family

Visit the Author Profile page at Harlequin.com for more titles.

Who shall separate us from the love of Christ?
Shall tribulation, or distress, or persecution,
or famine, or nakedness, or danger, or sword?
—*Romans* 8:35

To those who persevere.

To my family and friends,
for the support and prayers.

And to Melissa and Giselle.
Without you, I'd be a mess.
Thank you for everything!

Chapter One

From bodyguard to babysitter. Boone Wilder leaned against the exterior brick wall of a closed boutique store in a pricey part of Austin, Texas. The sun had set more than an hour earlier and the temperature had cooled to a balmy eighty degrees. Not bad for early September. But he wished he was at home in Martin's Crossing sipping iced tea on his front porch and not standing in front of a clothing store in Austin on a late-summer evening.

He should have argued a little more when his partner Daron McKay had asked him to take this case. Daron knew the subject and knew she wouldn't listen to him. The third partner at MWP Bodyguard Services, Lucy Palermo, was Boone's backup. Daron had joked that Lucy couldn't take lead because

Lucy would just shoot the client if she got on her nerves.

Lucy hadn't found that statement as amusing as Boone and Daron.

At the moment his client was across the street in a trendy café, sipping coffee and oblivious to his presence. That was how her dad, William Stanford, wanted it. Boone's job was to keep Kayla Stanford out of trouble, without her being aware. He'd been following her for a week now, close enough to keep her safe, far enough away that she didn't have a clue.

He'd like to keep it that way, with her not knowing of his existence. He was supposed to interfere in Kayla's life only if she appeared to be in danger, or if she appeared to be on the verge of creating a scandal. Those were her father's directives. Boone had talked to Kayla's half brother Brody Martin, who had assured him that she had a way of generating controversy.

A group of people were walking down the sidewalk. He stepped back, leaned against the wall and pulled his hat low. He touched the brim as they walked past, just to be gentlemanly. One of the women, a little older, and wearing too much makeup, winked and then grabbed the arm of a friend. They smiled and talked loudly about his jeans and cowboy boots, their voices echoing against the brick buildings on each side of the street.

As he watched for Kayla Stanford to leave the café, Boone planned what he'd say to Daron. Yeah, this was a good job and the big fat check they'd been paid was welcome. But this was not what Boone had signed on for when he, Daron and Lucy had started their bodyguard business a little over a year ago. So far they'd managed to build a decent business by protecting politicians and doing security at various functions. Those were the jobs they were trained for. The three of them had served together in Afghanistan and they'd formed a bond.

Kayla Stanford, half sister of the Martins of Martin's Crossing, was trouble. She needed a babysitter. Boone just didn't want to be that guy.

Unfortunately he was.

Across the street the neon open sign went off in the café. He headed down the sidewalk, keeping an eye on his target. The place was still lit up inside. Most of the customers had long since left and he could see Kayla standing near the door with a group of friends. Her dark hair was pulled up in one of those messy buns his sisters loved, and she wore a dark red dress that was too short. His granny would have told her some nice lace around the hem would look pretty. He grinned at the thought.

Then Kayla kissed cheeks, hugged friends and did a cutesy finger wave. As she walked out the door, her smile faded away. That didn't surprise him. He'd done some digging, talked to her family in Martin's Crossing, read some headlines. He'd learned a lot from the articles, from pictures in society columns. Most of the articles were about her antics, her beauty and her style. But he'd seen more. He'd noticed dark shadows under her eyes. He'd seen desperation. Everyone thought she had it all, but he thought she had less than most.

And she covered up her unhappiness by acting out. A couple of months ago, it was a slow-speed chase with the police.

The only time she kept to herself and stayed scandal-free was when she visited her siblings in Martin's Crossing. He'd never seen her in his hometown. She stayed at the ranch, holed up with her half sister Samantha Martin. Soon to be Samantha Jenkins.

Across the street she glanced around, and then walked down the sidewalk in the opposite direction. He'd guessed wrong. He'd thought she would cross the street and head for her car parked at the end of the block. When he glanced across the street, he noticed a shadow moving from the dark recesses of a building. Someone else seemed to be watching Kayla Stanford.

So much for an easy babysitting gig.

Someone was following her. Kayla walked faster, not taking time to glance back over her shoulder to see if she could get a look at the man. For two months, the feeling would come at the oddest times. The uneasy feeling as she walked down the street. The prickling of fear when she walked through the door of her apartment.

At first she'd convinced herself it was her imagination. And then she'd told herself it had to do with her lifestyle. She'd been partying hard for a few years, trying to numb herself against pain and anger. But a few months ago she'd quit everything, just to convince herself she was in her right mind and not imagining things.

The footsteps drew closer, speeding up to match her own hurried steps. She'd panicked when she first realized she'd gone in the opposite direction of her car. The farther she went, the darker it seemed to get. These weren't the streets she wanted to be on late at night, alone.

She reached into the purse that hung close to her waist. Her fingers curled around a small can. She turned, prepared to scream, to fight. Before she could do either, a fist connected with the side of her jaw. She jolted back, trying to stay upright. A rough shove and she fell backward, landing hard, her head hitting the brick building at her back. She caught a glimpse of blond hair and glasses. But the features were a blur.

Blinking, she fought to stay conscious. She heard a shout. Heard footsteps pounding. A hand reached for her arm. Unwilling to go down without a fight, she sat up, aimed and sprayed.

"Oh, man, you sprayed the wrong guy." The words sounded as if they were coming through a tunnel. She tried to focus but her eyes were burning and her head throbbed.

"Go away," she managed to croak out.

"Babysitting. I'm reduced to babysitting a woman who can't even spray the right man." Hands were on her arms. A face peered into hers. "Sorry, but I'm not going away."

"I'll spray you again." She meant for the

words to sound strong but they came out garbled and weak. She was still sitting on the sidewalk, her head resting on her knees. She took a deep breath that did nothing to ease the stabbing pain in her back and the headache that had clamped down on her skull.

"Take a deep breath," he ordered, ignoring her threats. Strong fingers felt her back. She winced. Those same fingers moved to her scalp. She let out a yelp. "Relax. And drop the pepper spray. I'm the rescuer, not the assailant. He's long gone."

She blinked a few times, trying to focus on the stranger looming over her. Tall and lean with ropy muscles, the man fit the "tall, dark and handsome" label to a T. He wore a dark cowboy hat, T-shirt and jeans. Something he'd said sank in. "Babysitting?"

"We've been hired by your father to keep track of you. And it looks as if you need us more than he realized."

"I can take care of myself." Her vision swam a little as she rubbed her jaw, wiggling it to make sure it wasn't broken.

"Of course you can take care of yourself. Do you know who that was?" he asked.

She shook her head and the movement cost

her. The pain radiated from her head down. Her stomach wasn't faring much better.

The man looming over her dialed his phone. "Lucy, can you pick us up? About two blocks down from the restaurant....No, I'm not fine. Neither is she. She's got a pretty good gash on the back of her head. And she sprayed me with pepper spray....Stop laughing. I'm going to have to take my contacts out so you'll have to drive us to the hospital."

After ending the call he swiped a finger across each eye and tossed contact lenses she couldn't see. But she did see that his eyes were watering and he tried to wipe the moisture with the tail of his shirt.

"Big baby," Kayla muttered. She felt a little bit sick. The world wasn't quite as sharp as it should have been. She wanted to tell him but she couldn't get the words out.

"Can you get up?"

He squatted next to her and peered at her face. His features swam. She tried to shake her head but that resulted in a wave of nausea. Something pressed against the back of her head. She tried to push his hand away but he couldn't be budged.

"You're bleeding," he said.

"I'm going to…" She didn't say more. The

world went dark and the last thing she remembered were strong arms picking her up as he yelled for Lucy to open the door.

Kayla came to as they were pulling up to the hospital. From a distance, she heard voices. They were discussing her father and being hired to keep her out of trouble. That was all she'd ever been to her father. Trouble. She struggled to sit up, pulling free from the arm that held her close.

"You're not trouble," he whispered. The words, the way he said them, took her by surprise. She wanted to believe him.

She sat up, closing her eyes when the world spun a little bit out of control. The back door opened and night air, humid and warm, clashed with the air-conditioned interior of the SUV.

"Come on, sunshine, let's get you checked out."

"How do I know you're not the one I should be afraid of?" She scooted toward the door where he stood.

He gave her a sympathetic look and she noticed that his eyes, dark brown and thick-lashed, were still red and watery from the pepper spray.

"I guess you'll have to trust me. As a rule, muggers don't typically take their victims to the emergency room." He reached for her, holding her steady when she wobbled. His hands were strong, calloused and strangely gentle.

"I'm going to park and I'll meet you inside," the woman driving the SUV called out. "Are you going to be okay, Boone?"

"I can't see much but other than that, great. Don't be too long," her rescuer responded.

"Your name is Boone?" Kayla asked as he led her toward the entrance of the ER.

"Boone Wilder."

"I've heard that name before." She had to stop for a second. Her head was pounding and she felt sick.

"I'm from Martin's Crossing." He slipped his hand from hers and put an arm around her back. "Are you going to make it?"

"Of course. I don't even need to be here."

"I think we'll get a second opinion on that."

"I could refuse treatment," she said as they headed up the sidewalk toward the entrance.

"Yeah, you could. But it's hard to refuse treatment if you're unconscious."

"How did you become my babysitter, Boone Wilder?" She blinked away the blurriness and kept walking, aware that he was studying her as if he thought she might fall over.

"Your father hired our bodyguard service to keep you out of trouble for the duration of this election. I don't think he realized you were actually in need of a bodyguard. Any idea who that was back there?"

"Not a clue."

"But since you were armed with pepper spray, I'm guessing this wasn't random?"

"It's been going on for a couple of months." She stopped as another wave of dizziness hit, making her vision swim.

Without warning she was scooped into his arms. Again.

"You don't have to carry me," she protested, albeit weakly.

"No, of course not. But I also don't want you passing out in the parking lot. Relax. You're not as light as you look."

"Charming."

He flashed white teeth and a dimple. "I try."

She felt him limp a bit as they headed toward the door. "I can walk."

"Probably."

To distract herself she studied his face. Lean and handsome, but rugged. She had never been attracted to the type. As she perused his features she noticed a scar on his cheek. It was a few inches long and jagged. There was a similar scar on his neck, just above his collarbone. Without thinking, she touched it.

He flinched.

"I'm sorry. What happened?" She pulled back, suddenly unsure.

"Nothing personal," he growled. "But it isn't any of your business."

"Of course it isn't. I'd love to tell you my life isn't any of your business. But I guess my dad has taken that right from me."

"And if we hadn't been there tonight?"

She shivered and his arms tightened. They walked through the doors of the ER and he settled her in a wheelchair that had been left near the entrance. She brought her legs up and huddled tight to warm herself. Boone pushed her to the front desk. There were questions to answer, paperwork to fill out, and then they were directed through double doors where a nurse met them.

"Right this way." The nurse motioned them to follow her to a room midway down the hall.

"She's cold. Can you get her a blanket?" Boone said as he pushed her into the room.

"I should call your dad," he said to her.

"Don't bother." Kayla blinked away tears

that she told herself were the result of the blow to her head and nothing more. "He's out of town."

"Still," he said, sounding insistent. She wished he'd go away. But if he did, she'd be alone. She was tired of being alone.

What did that say about her life, that she was so lonely she wanted this man, this stranger, to stay with her? There was something comforting about his presence.

"I'll call your sister, then," he said. He pulled off his cowboy hat and brushed a hand through short, dark hair. His eyes still watered.

"You should get your eyes cleaned out," Kayla offered.

The nurse gave him a good look as she helped Kayla onto the bed. "I'll have an aid flush your eyes out. Right now let's get you settled. I'll be right back and we'll get you changed into a gown."

Kayla gripped the edge of the bed as another wave of dizziness hit. "I'm sorry you've been dragged into this. And for the pepper spray. I'll pay to replace your contacts."

"No need to apologize." His voice rumbled close by. She felt his hand on her foot. He was removing her shoes. First one and then the other. She forced her eyes open and watched him. He was looking down so she had a view of the crown of his head, of his dark hair.

"Thank you." She managed to get the words out, closing her eyes again to block his concerned expression and the tumultuous emotions that bounced around inside her.

Needing someone was not her thing.

"You're welcome," he said, standing up. "Is there anything else I can do?"

She shook her head, the movement costing her. She put a hand to her temple. "Make this headache go away?"

He put a hand on her shoulder briefly. "I'm sure they'll give you something."

And then he was moving toward the door and the nurse was there, agreeing that they would get her something for pain.

"I can't," Kayla tried to explain. The nurse gave her a curious look. "No narcotics."

Boone Wilder, babysitter, bodyguard, whatever he thought of himself, stopped at the door. "I'll be here when you get back from CT. And we'll have to call the police and file a report."

The door slid open and his partner stepped inside. She wasn't tall but Kayla got the impression this woman with her long dark hair, dark eyes and pretty face could intimidate almost anyone.

"Kayla Stanford, this is Lucy Palermo. We're partners in MPW Bodyguard services." Boone waved at the other woman in introduction.

"Palermo. Wilder. What does the M stand for?" Kayla asked as she leaned back on the bed.

"McKay. Daron McKay," Boone said.

"Of course." She covered her eyes with her hand to block the bright fluorescent lighting. "Our dads have worked together in the past."

"That's what Daron told us," Lucy said with just the slightest Hispanic accent.

The nurse rested a hand on Kayla's arm. "Time to get you into that hospital gown."

"We'll be out in the hall," Boone said as he settled his hat back on his head.

"You don't have to stay," Kayla shot back, knowing he wouldn't listen.

"You can't get rid of us that easily."

Of course she couldn't. And even though she'd said the words, she didn't mean them. Even strangers who had been paid to keep tabs on her were better than nothing.

She was so tired of being alone.

Chapter Two

Sunshine streamed through the bedroom window of her apartment. Kayla closed her eyes and wished away the brightness. Worse, someone was singing. She put a hand to her head where it ached. Minor concussion, staples in the back of her head and a bruise on her shoulder. The doctor last night had told her she was fortunate. It could have been worse.

The police report they'd taken after the CT scan and stitches had furthered that theory. They wrote it off as an attempted mugging. She'd allowed them to think so. Fortunately Boone Wilder hadn't been around to add his opinion.

But he was here now. She was sure it was him singing about sunshine.

She groaned, rolled over and gingerly pushed

herself to a sitting position on the edge of her bed.

"Welcome back to the land of the living." Lucy Palermo's softly accented voice took her by surprise.

Kayla turned and saw her sitting in the chair in the corner, a book in her lap. Her dark hair was braided and she wore a T-shirt and yoga pants.

"I suppose that's a good thing," Kayla said as she stood. "Oh, wow, standing is over-rated."

"Take it easy." Lucy rushed to Kayla's side.

"I'm not going to fall." Kayla took a deep breath. "I'm going to take a shower."

"I'll be here if you need anything."

"I don't need anything," Kayla said, then she sighed, because it wasn't the other woman's fault. "I'm a grown woman and I should have a say in whether or not I allow body-guards to follow me."

Lucy shrugged. "I agree. Unfortunately that isn't up to me."

The singing grew louder, and Kayla cringed. "Does he have to sing?"

"Yeah, unfortunately he does. You'll get used to it. Or buy earplugs."

She made it to the door of the bathroom

but hesitated at the opening. "Is that bacon I smell?"

Lucy rolled her dark eyes. "Yeah, he insists on a big breakfast every morning. Do you want to eat before you shower?"

"No, that's okay. I'm not hungry."

Dark eyes swept her from top to bottom. "You might not be hungry, but you look as though you haven't had a decent meal in weeks."

"I don't think my dad hired you to make sure I eat."

"No, I guess he didn't." Lucy opened her book and let the subject drop.

Kayla didn't want food. She closed her eyes and counted to ten as she leaned against the door frame. But she'd have to count to a million to get through this, through strangers in her home, through the fear that stalked her every day, through the cravings that still dogged her at times. Through the emotional roller coaster of losing the mother she hadn't ever really known. Could you lose someone you never had?

The aroma of breakfast invaded her senses. The bacon smelled so good. She tried to remember the last time she'd had a decent breakfast, something other than a doughnut and coffee. Or just coffee. She couldn't remember.

"I'll be out in ten minutes," she told Lucy as she closed the door behind her.

Fifteen minutes later she emerged. Boone Wilder in jeans, a T-shirt, cowboy hat and no shoes was standing in her kitchen at the sink washing dishes. She glanced past him, to the full pot of coffee, the plate of biscuits and the pan of gravy.

He tossed her a smile over his shoulder. "Hey, sunshine, 'bout time you crawled out of bed."

She glanced at the clock. Barely eight in the morning. "It isn't as if I slept until noon."

"No, I guess not. Grab some breakfast. We have a lot to do today."

Her mouth watered. She shook her head. "I don't eat breakfast."

He looked at her in mock horror. "What? It's the most important meal of the day."

Was he always this cheerful? She shook her head and ignored the tantalizing aroma that filled her kitchen. She rarely cooked, and if she did it was a frozen dinner, something on the grill or takeout reheated in the microwave. Boone Wilder was filling a plate with biscuits, gravy and bacon.

He shoved the plate into her hands and nodded toward the seat on the other side of the counter. "Eat."

She lifted the plate to inhale. "You made this?"

"Of course."

She took a seat on the opposite side of the counter. "What is it we have to do today?"

He poured her a cup of coffee and slid it across the counter. "First, I need a tux."

"Why, are you going to a wedding?" She eyed him over the rim of her coffee mug. She hoped he was the best man, not the groom.

"Nope, I'm taking you to the ball, Cinderella."

"Sorry, but no. I'm not fond of the wicked stepmother."

"But I'd make such a snazzy Prince Charming," he said as he lifted his coffee cup in salute. "Do you have something against the prince, the singing animals or wicked stepmothers?"

"All of the above." She gave him a long look that forced a sharp comment. "Especially handsome princes with cowboy hats and big smiles."

"Ouch." He touched his hand to his heart. "Sorry, but we don't have a choice."

"Then, tell me what we're really doing because I'm too old for fairy tales."

"We're going to your dad's fund-raiser. I'm supposed to make sure you show up and that you behave."

She took a bite of biscuit. "He knows me so well."

That was what this was all about. It wasn't about her safety. It was about his campaign. His career. And making sure she didn't mess up either one. She was twenty-four years old and he still doubted her ability to be a Stanford. Truth be told, she doubted it, too. If he hadn't done the DNA test, she would have been positive she wasn't his offspring, so different were they.

She was her mother's daughter. The embarrassment. He'd never actually called her that. Her youngest half brother, Michael, had. She'd heard him tell a friend to ignore her, that she was dropped off on the doorstep as a baby and her mother was insane.

"You okay?" Boone Wilder's voice was softly concerned, taking her by surprise.

She looked up from the empty plate and gave him her best carefree smile. "Of course. I'm just deciding what to wear."

"Of course you are."

"We could let him know I have a concussion and maybe he'll let us off the hook."

"I already tried that. He said if you can walk, he wants you there."

"Of course he did. Dear old Dad, he's all heart."

He refilled her mug, then his. "For what it's worth, he did sound concerned."

"Did he?" That was a surprise. She carried her plate to the sink and rinsed it. "Where's Lucy?"

"On your patio. She said you have the best view in the city." Boone took the rinsed plate and opened the door of the dishwasher.

"I'm sorry about last night. I'm sure you didn't plan for a fun Friday night at the ER."

"We were working. So nothing to apologize for."

Of course. Her dad was probably paying them a decent amount for their babysitting services. "If you have your measurements, we can send out for a tux. No need to go shopping. And I already have a dress."

"I do have my measurements. But I'd give anything to not go shopping."

She noticed he rubbed his shoulder as he said it. Her gaze was drawn again to the scar on his face, and then lower to the one on his neck.

"Shrapnel," he said.

She met his dark gaze. "I'm sorry, I didn't mean to stare."

"No one ever does."

"Iraq?"

"Afghanistan." He set his cup on the counter. "About that monkey suit I have to wear…"

She nodded and headed for her room and her cell phone she'd left there. When she walked through the door of her bedroom, she noticed the bouquet of flowers on her dresser. Her dad had probably sent them. His way of being there when he wasn't.

She found the card buried amid the blooms and opened it.

You shouldn't have run, because now we're going to play dirty. Your secrets remain secrets. We get the money. Tell your father.

She grabbed the flowers and hurried from her room, carrying them in front of her. She ignored Boone as she opened the trash can and shoved the flowers inside, vase and all. She ripped up the card and tossed it in, shuddering as the scraps of paper fluttered among the bloodred blooms.

"What's that all about?" Boone's voice

rumbled in her ear. She shook her head, unable to answer.

He reached past her, retrieving the pieces of card.

"Who delivered these?" he asked as he pieced the card together on the counter.

"Like I know? I was sleeping. You were here when they were delivered." Her voice shook. She really didn't want to sound shaky or afraid. She didn't want to give this unknown person that kind of power over her.

"No, actually, I wasn't. The flowers were on your dresser when we got here last night. You were pretty wiped out and probably didn't notice."

"They were in here already?"

"Yeah, darlin', they were here. On your dresser. You didn't know you had flowers?"

"No. I didn't know."

"Well, that's a problem," Boone said, as casual as if he was talking about the weather.

"So what do we do?" Lucy asked as she walked in from the living room.

"We go on about our business." Boone shrugged as he said it. "And we all sit down and get honest about what's going on here. Your dad said he wants you front and center at campaign events. And you're trying to push this off as an overzealous admirer. Neither of you is being honest. What secrets is this guy talking about?"

"I don't know. Maybe my drug use. Most people know about my mom. Maybe this person believes there's more to her story. I don't know."

"I'm not buying any of it." Boone grabbed a ziplock bag out of a drawer and brushed the pieces of note into it. "We'll see if we can salvage any prints."

"I didn't know that they were contacting my dad," Kayla said. She tried to remember something, anything about her attacker.

"He wanted to protect you. You were obviously trying to protect him," Lucy chimed in.

"Yes, we're all about protecting one another." Kayla walked away, unwilling to dwell on the pain of knowing how untrue those words were.

Boone followed her out to the deck. She walked to the ledge and looked out over the city of Austin. It was an incredible view. She blinked back tears that threatened to blur her vision. She would not cry.

A hand, strong and warm, rested on her shoulder, pulled her a little bit close, then moved away. She found herself wanting to slide close to him, to allow the comfort of his touch to continue. She could use a hug right now.

Great, she was getting sappy. She could imagine the look on his face if she told him she needed a hug. He'd get that goofy grin on his face and pull the Prince-Charming-to-the-rescue act. No, she didn't need that.

Take a deep breath. Blink away the tears. Be the Kayla people expected.

"We should order that tux now. Wouldn't want to disappoint my father and show up in jeans and boots. And ruin his black tie affair."

He laughed. "No, we wouldn't want to do that. Glad you're back, Stanford. I would miss this sweet sarcasm if it got all mixed up with other emotions."

"Yes, I do like predictable."

He tipped back his black cowboy hat and winked. "Predictable is one thing you're not."

That evening Lucy drove them to the clubhouse of the Summer Springs Country Club. "I'll be waiting out here for you all. Try not to get in trouble."

"Because Lucy doesn't want to have to shoot anyone," Boone quipped, hoping to lighten the mood. He winked at his partner and she grinned back. "We'll be good, Luce. And keep an eye out for our blond and handsome friend who likes to leave roses and concussions as a calling card."

"Will do, partner."

Boone opened the door and then stepped back to allow his date to exit the vehicle. She wore a black evening dress, with pearls around her neck and all that dark hair pulled back in some kind of fancy bun.

"You clean up pretty good, Kayla Stanford." He offered her his arm and she settled her fingers on the crook of his elbow. "You smell good, too."

"Charming."

"That's *Prince* Charming to you."

She sighed. "Are you ever serious?"

"I thought you were cornering the market on serious. And I have to say, I'm a little disappointed. You're not living up to your reputation."

"I'm turning over a new leaf," she offered. He didn't push. He'd seen the book for the twelve-step program in her apartment, worn with pages dog-eared. He got it. They all had stuff they had to battle.

"Well, then, let's do this." He led her toward the entrance of the stone-and-stucco building.

People were milling about at the entrance. Security checked IDs at the door.

Kayla tightened her grip on his arm.

"You okay?"

She nodded and kept walking. "I'm good. I really dislike these functions. I always feel like I don't belong. You know, square, square, square, oval."

"You're the oval?"

A hint of a smile tilted her pretty lips. "Yeah, that's me."

"Well, tonight you're with another oval. Have a little faith, Kayla."

"Faith?" She smiled at that. "Now you sound like the Martins."

"They're good people."

"Yes, they are. They've all accepted me. Helped me."

"If the Martins like you, then you've got decent people in your corner." He patted the hand on his elbow.

She shot him a look. "Let's not get all emotional, cowboy. You're my bodyguard, not my therapist."

"You got that right." Boone took a quick look around. Because he was her bodyguard, not a therapist. And definitely not her date.

This wasn't new territory for him, slipping

into the role of fixer. He'd learned a few hard lessons on that, the most important one in Afghanistan. He had the scars as a reminder.

He tried to remember the rules. Don't get taken in by sad stories, by soft looks or a pretty face. Definitely don't get personal with a client.

He had his own family to worry about. They needed him present in their lives, not sidetracked. Kayla needed him unemotional if he was going to keep her safe.

At the door the security detail checked their names against the list of invited guests. Boone let out a low whistle as they were ushered inside.

"Don't be too impressed," Kayla warned.

"I'm not impressed, I just didn't realize money could be wasted this way. I bet I could fence our entire property with the money they spent on these light fixtures."

She looked up, blinking, as if she'd never noticed those fancy crystal fixtures before. "I guess you probably could. We could take one with us, if you'd like?"

He laughed. "There's the Kayla I've heard so much about. What do we do first?"

"Socialize," she said. "I'm sure everyone is mingling, discussing politics and their neighbors and how to take down the person they pretend is their best friend."

"Sounds like a great time. I can't believe you don't enjoy these events."

She flicked a piece of lint off the collar of his tuxedo and smiled up at him. "I find ways to enjoy myself."

The statement, casual with a hint of a grin and a mischievous twinkle in her blue eyes, sounded warning bells. He gave her a careful look and she widened those same blue eyes in a less-than-perfect imitation of innocence.

"Not tonight," he warned.

"Spoilsport."

"No, just the guy who wants to keep you safe. I can't do that if you pull a stunt."

"I'm not going to do anything, I promise. Come with me. Time to greet my father."

She led him through double doors and into a large room complete with linen-covered tables, candlelight, a small orchestra in the far corner and of course dozens of people. Boone took a careful look around the room. So these were the people who paid hundreds of dollars a plate just to say they'd attended or contributed. Impressive.

"There's my father." She nodded in the direction of a stately gray-haired man, his tuxedo obviously not rented.

"Should we make our presence known?"

"Soon. He's talking to supporters. The woman coming up behind him is my stepmother, Marietta. My half brother Andrew is talking to that group. He's very good at being good."

She said it in such a way that meant she didn't dislike Andrew. As if his being good wasn't a horrible thing.

"We should mingle, correct?" Boone put a hand to her back and guided her around the room. She froze beneath his touch as he headed her toward a table of drinks.

"No, let's not. Please."

"There's iced tea and lemonade."

"It isn't about the drinks, Wilder. It's just… there are people here I prefer to avoid. At all costs."

"Okay. Would any of them be the one who is stalking you?" He settled his gaze on the table, on the people gathered. Most were older men, a few women. He didn't see anyone who should make her panic.

She took in a deep breath and gave a quick look around the room. "No one in that group. But I'd prefer to avoid them all the same."

"Kayla, you're here," a woman called out. Kayla turned, straightening as she did. Poised but trembling.

The stepmother was bearing down on them. Marietta Stanford was tall with pale blond hair, a pinched mouth and less-than-friendly gray eyes. Boone didn't know much about this world, but to his inexperienced eye he'd call her expensive and high maintenance.

"Of course I am. I couldn't very well stay home, could I, Mother?"

Marietta Stanford's nostrils flared. "Don't start."

Kayla smiled. "Right, I forgot. My father wanted me here. So I'm here."

Boone moved a little closer, offering the protection of his nearness. That wasn't his job, but if he was going to protect someone, he'd protect from all corners.

"Try to show some class tonight," Marietta warned. And then she smiled, as if they'd been talking about the weather. "The pearls are a lovely touch."

"For what it's worth, I think she has the market cornered on class." Boone winked at Kayla and was rewarded with a smile.

They moved away from her stepmother.

"Thank you," Kayla whispered.

"No problem. Everyone needs someone in their corner."

She nodded. "That's a novel idea. If you'll excuse me, I'm going to the restroom."

"You're okay?"

"Of course," she said as they maneuvered through the room.

For the next five minutes he stood at the door waiting for Kayla to reappear. He glanced at his watch, then smiled at the group of women who gave him cautious looks as they walked in and out.

Finally he called Lucy. "She escaped."

Lucy laughed. "Already?"

"She said she needed to use the restroom. I've been waiting here for a long time. People are starting to stare."

"I'll walk around back. See if you can get someone to go in. Maybe she's just hiding in there."

"Yeah, I will. Stay on the line."

He looked around and as he did he caught a glimpse of a familiar profile.

"Luce, see if you can find her pronto. We have trouble in here. A certain blond with glasses."

"Will do."

As he hurried across the room, someone grabbed his arm, bringing him to a dead stop.

"Boone Wilder?" The older man had a firm grip, Boone would give him that.

"Yes, sir. You must be Mr. Stanford."

"I am. And where's my daughter?"

"She's in the restroom. But, sir, I just saw the man who attacked her last night. If you don't mind having this conversation later…"

"What? Where?" William Stanford glanced around. So did Boone. There were several hundred people in attendance and it seemed that half of them were gathered in the lobby.

"Great. He's gone."

"Of course he is. Or he never existed. My daughter has a wild imagination. This isn't the first story she's created and it won't be the last."

"The attack last night wasn't her imagination. The concussion and the bruise on her jaw are not imaginary." Boone continued to watch the crowd. He briefly looked at his client. "And the letters the two of you are getting, letters you failed to divulge, are not imaginary."

A flicker of concern briefly settled in Mr. Stanford's eyes. "She's getting them, too?"

"Yes, she is. I don't want to jump to conclusions but I think there might have been more to last night's attack. It could be that their next step is to kidnap your daughter. Someone has something on you other than your daughter's very public behavior. You'd best figure out what it is."

Another man approached them, tall with graying hair and sharp, dark eyes. Boone guessed him to be in his late forties.

"Boone Wilder, this is my law partner and campaign manager, Paul Whitman," William Stanford said.

"Mr. Whitman." Boone shook his hand. It was a little too soft and a little too snaky. He refocused on his client. "I'm going to ask that you excuse your daughter from this event."

"Has something happened to our little Kayla?" Mr. Whitman asked in a voice that matched his snaky appearance. "She does tend to fabricate stories."

Boone caught a quick look between the two men. And Mr. Stanford's was a definite warning to the other man.

"Being attacked isn't a story," Boone defended Kayla for the second time.

"Then, I'm going to ask that you keep my

daughter not only out of trouble but out of harm's way. I don't want her hurt."

"We might need to remove her from Austin." Boone looked down at his phone and the text from Lucy. She had Kayla.

"I need my family around me during this election, Wilder."

"Yes, sir. But you also hired me to keep your daughter safe. That's my priority here, not your campaign."

Someone called out and Mr. Stanford raised a hand to put them off. "I agree. But before you take her anywhere, you let me know. If you can't reach me, then leave a message at my office, or let Paul know."

No, Boone didn't think he'd be leaving any messages with Paul Whitman. "I'll let you know. For now, though, we're leaving this event."

"Where is my daughter, Mr. Wilder?"

"With my partner, Lucy Palermo. They're outside in the vehicle and waiting for me."

"Then, you should go," he said. "Keep her safe, Wilder."

"I'll do my best."

Boone headed out to the waiting SUV. He

got in the backseat. Kayla was in the front. She didn't turn to look at him.

"Nice move, Stanford. Did you go out the window?"

"Not now, Boone." Lucy drove away from the building.

"Why not now? She's in danger and rather than staying safe, she's jumping out windows so she doesn't have to go to Daddy's fancy dinner party."

Lucy shot him a meaningful look. "Not. Now."

He raised both hands in surrender. "Fine, not now."

That was when he realized there were tears streaming down Kayla's cheeks. He sighed and leaned back in his seat, but he was far from relaxed. Protecting Kayla Stanford was supposed to be an easy job. Keep her out of trouble and make sure she showed up on time for her father's campaign events.

He hadn't considered she'd need a friend more than she needed a bodyguard.

Chapter Three

Kayla woke up early Monday morning. She blamed her new schedule on the cowboy and his partner, who had taken up residence in her apartment. They kept country hours, in bed shortly after ten and up by six in the morning.

She enjoyed sleeping in. If she didn't sleep late, there would be too many hours in a day to live, to think, to try to be happy. And to fail. Her dad had asked her to go to work for him, to use her college degree in prelaw. He'd suggested teaching if she didn't want that. She didn't want any part of her father's world. She knew it too well, knew the underhanded dealings and the backstabbing.

She tiptoed out of her room, leaving Lucy asleep on the cot she'd insisted on. Boone was asleep on her couch, stretched out, arm over his face, and snoring. She pinched his nose closed to stop the racket.

He jumped up off the sofa, gasping and flailing.

"Are you trying to kill me?"

She laughed. "No, I just wanted you to stop snoring."

"That was a definite attempt on my life. And I don't snore." He glanced at his watch. "Why are you up so early?"

"Because my apartment has been invaded and I can no longer sleep late."

"Tough, Stanford. Go back to sleep so I can sleep late."

"You don't sleep late," she accused.

"Sometimes I do. Today is one of those days."

"Too bad, because today is a day I'd like to go shopping and maybe grab some lunch."

"Have fun with that."

"You're my date," she shot back.

"No, I'm your bodyguard. There's a difference. And I think shopping is dangerous for my health."

"I need ranch clothes because you seem to think I'm going to have to be removed from Austin." She sat down in the chair across from him as he leaned back and brushed a hand through his short dark hair.

"I've seen your closet. You don't need clothes."

"Maybe not, but I can't take another day cooped up inside. Lucy has to run to Stephenville today to check on her mom. So I'm stuck with you. And we're going shopping."

"Can I have coffee at least?"

"Yes, you can have coffee. I'll even prove my worth by making it. I do know how to do a few things."

He gave her a serious look. "Stanford, I'm not the one who doubts your abilities. You are."

"Great, we're getting Freudian again. I'll make the coffee and you climb back under the rock you crawled out of."

He groaned and stood. "I was happy under that rock."

He followed her to the kitchen, and as she started the coffee, he rummaged through the refrigerator. "I should have gone to the store."

"I have toaster pastries in the cabinet," she told him.

"I'm not a fan of starting my morning with pure sugar."

She slid the sugar jar down the counter and grinned. "Go for it, it might sweeten you up."

The doorbell rang. He glanced at her, all cowboy, sleepy and a little bit grumpy. A dark brow shot up. He pushed himself away from the counter and headed for the front door. She watched from the safety of the kitchen as he looked through the peephole.

"Who is it?"

He put a finger to his lips and pointed toward the bedroom. She obeyed, even though she wanted to stay, not only to see who it was, but because he shouldn't be left alone. But the look on his face told her she shouldn't argue.

Lucy was just waking up when Kayla walked into the room.

"Who's here?" she asked, brushing long hair from her face.

Kayla peeked out the door but Lucy pushed it closed. "I'm not sure who it is," she admitted.

"Then, I doubt Boone wants your head sticking out." Then Lucy was strapping on a sidearm and slipping out of the room, leaving Kayla very much alone and in the dark.

Minutes later the door opened and Lucy peeked in.

"All clear."

"Who was it?" Kayla asked as she followed the other woman to the kitchen.

"Absolutely no one," Lucy answered as she poured herself a cup of coffee. She took a sip and frowned. "Did you make this?"

"Yes."

"Don't ever do that again." Lucy poured the coffee down the drain. "There wasn't anyone at the door. There was a letter."

"Where's Boone?"

"Checking the building."

Kayla headed for the door. "Alone?"

"What do you think you're doing?" Lucy followed, pulling her back before she could reach for the doorknob.

"I want to make sure he's okay."

"And this is how it starts," Lucy said with an exaggerated roll of her dark brown eyes. "He's got pretty eyes, they say. He's a gentleman, they sigh."

"I don't care about his eyes. I'd rather him not get shot in my building." Kayla went back to the kitchen. "It would make a mess in the hallway."

Lucy laughed. "I'm not sure I like you, but you're okay."

She was used to people not really liking her. But for some reason, this hurt more than usual.

"Boone can take care of himself," Lucy continued. "He's smart and he's well trained."

The front door opened. Kayla didn't look, because if she looked Lucy would draw conclusions that weren't accurate. It wasn't his eyes, his smile or anything else. As she poured more water into the coffeemaker, she realized she didn't know what it was about Boone. She didn't really want to delve into it because it might cost her.

"I'm not sure how they're slipping out of here, but they're gone." He limped as he headed for a seat at the bar.

"You okay?" Lucy asked, as she finished making the coffee that Kayla had started.

He arched a dark brow at her.

"And you have the letter?" Kayla asked, not asking about his health. It was obviously a topic he wanted to avoid.

He pulled on latex gloves and held the letter up for Kayla to see. "Recognize that handwriting?"

"It's the same as the other letters. I don't know who it belongs to."

He slid a knife under the seal and pulled out a letter and a picture. His brows drew together as he read and his mouth tugged at the corner. Was he laughing at this, as if it were a game?

"It isn't funny, Wilder. This is my life."

He held up a picture. "Care to explain why you were crossing the border, princess?"

She leaned against the counter and buried her face in her hands. Next to her Lucy snickered. Kayla didn't blame her. If she wasn't so humiliated, she'd laugh, too. In the past she would have laughed with them. It was all a big joke. But not really. In truth it was her way of striking back at her father for hurting her.

"Well?" His voice was soft, luring her out of her thoughts.

"It was after my mom died. I went to Mexico. Two weeks of stupidity. I was slowly killing myself, intentionally, unintentionally, I'm not sure. I lost my passport."

"You could have called Daddy," Lucy said.

"I could have, but what fun would there have been in that? A friend stayed behind with me. We met some people. And somehow we ended up being smuggled across the border. The rest of our group met up with us and brought us home."

"You really think that's a game?" Lucy said sharply.

"No, it isn't a game. I'd like to think I'm a somewhat better person now. I'm still working on it, though."

Lucy raised both hands. "Yeah, okay. What about the letter, Boone?"

He spread it out on the counter. "It's a warning. Requesting the first payment or the story gets leaked to the press. And it warns us not to let you out of our sight."

"What do I do now?"

Boone slid the note back inside the envelope. "It's time to go to the police with this information. I know your father wants to keep it quiet, but someone tried to hurt you. That same someone has followed you. They've been in your apartment."

"He isn't going to agree with you," Kayla warned. "This is stuff he'd like to keep private and someone wants to make it public. Going to the police..."

"Might stop them. If it's made public, they'll stop trying to get money for secrets that are no longer secrets. Or scandals that aren't scandals, but public knowledge."

Kayla walked away, taking the darkest of her secrets with her, away from the prying eyes of two people who didn't care, not about her. They cared about doing their jobs. They cared enough to keep her safe. But her past was hers. As angry as she was with her father, she wouldn't let other people destroy him.

"Hey, we have to deal with this." Boone followed her to the deck. The sun was beating down and the concrete was hot under her feet. She sat down and he pulled up another chair to sit facing her.

"I'm not going to the police," she said, determined to have her way in this.

"We don't have a choice. I'm going to call your dad and he'll back me up on this. I don't know what it is between the two of you, but I'm pretty sure you both care more than you let on."

"Yes, we care." She looked away, to the potted palm in the corner and the flowerpot that she'd picked up at a discount store because it looked cheerful. She didn't know what it was called or how she'd managed to keep it alive.

"Are there more letters?"

She shook her head. "I threw them away. At first I just thought it was a nuisance. But then I started feeling as if I was being followed, and I'm sure they've been in my apartment more than once."

"And your dad has gotten letters, too?"

"Yeah, he's gotten letters."

He leaned back in the chair and stretched his jean-clad legs in front of him. "Well, Kayla, I guess it's time we headed for Martin's Crossing."

"Why?"

"Because I know I can keep you safe there while the police try to figure out who's blackmailing your dad."

"You can keep me safe here," she insisted, not liking the pleading tone in her voice.

"I can keep you safer on my own turf."

Martin's Crossing. She shouldn't have minded the idea of going to the place her siblings called home. But she wasn't a Martin of Martin's Crossing. She was their half sister. The only thing they had in common was the mother who had abandoned them all.

"I guess refusing to go won't work."

He laughed at that. "'Fraid not. Before long you'll be wishing I was the only Wilder in your life."

By ten o'clock that evening Boone and Kayla were heading for the Wilder Ranch. Lucy had been turned loose to head home for a few days.

Exhausted by a day that had included police reports and long conversations with her father, Kayla slept the ride away, which helped her avoid answering any more of Boone's questions. She didn't want to explain the things best left in the past. Those subjects were walls between herself and her father. Lack of trust loomed as the largest barrier in their ever-fragile relationship.

She didn't want Boone inside those walls.

She woke up as they drove through Martin's Crossing. Her head had been at a strange angle and her neck ached. She rubbed it, aware that Boone had probably seen her drool in her sleep.

"We're home," he said, his voice softly husky in the dark interior of the truck.

Home. It wasn't her home, even though it had become familiar to her in the past year. The main street where her brother Duke owned Duke's No Bar and Grill. Across the street was the shop his wife, Oregon, owned, Oregon's All Things. Duke's wife was crafty and artistic. She made clothes, hand-painted Christmas ornaments and other pretty items. The grocery store was to the right of Oregon's. Lefty Mueller's store, where he sold wooden Christmas carousels and other hand-carved art, was to the left. Kayla was a city girl but Martin's Crossing held a certain appeal. But not long-term. Not for her.

For some reason the thought invoked a melancholy that took her by surprise, sending a few tears trickling down her cheeks. She kept her gaze on the passing scenery and brushed away the tears.

"Where do your parents live?" she asked, turning from the window and pulling her hair back from her face.

"A few minutes out of town." He kept driving, the radio playing country music and the open windows letting in warm summer air. "You okay?"

"Of course."

He cleared his throat, then let out a heartfelt sigh. "You were crying."

"I wasn't."

"I have sisters, I know tears of sadness, tears of frustration. All brands of tears."

"Okay, Mr. Tear Expert, why was I crying?"

"I'm not sure of the exact reason, but if you want to talk…"

"I'd rather not."

"Sometimes it helps," he prodded.

"Really? I don't see you wearing your heart on your sleeve."

"No, I guess I don't."

She stared out the open window, enjoying the humid breeze that lifted hair that had come loose. Outside the landscape was dark except for an occasional security light that flashed an orange glow across a lawn or outbuilding and the silvery light of a nearly full moon. Cattle were dark silhouettes grazing in the fields.

They turned up a narrow, rutted driveway. Ahead she could see a two-story white farmhouse. The front-porch light was on. In the distance she could see the dark shapes that meant numerous outbuildings.

"I hope you don't mind the country."

"It isn't my favorite."

He laughed a little. "Well, you'll either sink or swim, sunshine."

Sunshine. She'd never had a nickname. She'd never been anyone's sunshine. It didn't mean anything to him. But it meant something to her. Something that she couldn't quite define.

Sunshine was definitely better than Cinderella.

"Here we are. Home sweet home. I promise

you, you're in for a real experience. We are a pretty crazy bunch."

"I can handle it."

"I'm sure you can." He got out of the truck, and she followed.

He held her suitcase and handed her the smaller overnight bag that accompanied it. "Let's get you settled."

"Don't you live here?"

He shook his head. "No. I bought a little RV. It's hooked up to power over by the barn."

"But you're going to be close by, right?" She felt as if he was suddenly drifting out of reach. She took a deep breath. He was practically a stranger. Not her lifeline.

"I'll be around more than you can stand. But I prefer my own space. I'm not much for company and big crowds. Believe me, you're going to have your share of people. You'll want solitude when you're done with this month on the Wilder Ranch."

"Month?"

He shrugged it off. "We aren't sending you out on your own until we know who is behind the threats and the attack. Maybe it wasn't the same guy."

"I kind of think it is."

She followed him up the steps and as they

got to the front door, it opened. Standing on the other side of the screen door was a woman past middle age. Her dark hair was short and framed a classically beautiful face.

"You must be Kayla," the woman said, an almost imperceptible Hispanic accent, giving the words a soft lilt. "I'm Maria Wilder."

"Mrs. Wilder, thank you for letting me stay with you."

Boone's mother laughed. "Don't thank me yet. You haven't met everyone."

Boone opened the door and motioned Kayla inside. She glanced back, worried he wouldn't go in with her. But he did. The lifeline was intact.

"I'm putting you upstairs in Boone's old room. Janie is just down the hall from you with Essie and Allie. Michaela is across the hall. Jase and Lucas are on the other side of her. We're downstairs if you need anything."

"I'm sure I'll be fine. I'm so sorry for putting you out this way," she started to explain.

Maria Wilder waved a hand. "Don't be silly. We don't mind."

She led Kayla up the stairs to a bedroom that was small but bright and airy. A quilt covered the twin bed. A rocking chair nearby had another quilt folded over the arm. Braided rugs in soft spring colors were scattered on the wood floor.

"It isn't much but it's clean. And most of Boone's smelly past has been evicted. Shoes, clothes, high school uniforms that got shoved in corners and forgotten." Maria Wilder turned down the blanket on the bed.

"It's perfect."

Boone's mother gave her a quick hug. "Are you hungry?"

"Prepare to be fattened up, Stanford."

His mother swatted at his arm. "Behave. No one likes to go to bed hungry. And young ladies don't like to be told they need to be 'fattened up.'"

"I'm fine, but thank you. We grabbed fast food on our way."

Maria made a face. "Bah. Fast food isn't real food."

"Really, I'm fine. But thank you. I'm looking forward to a good night's sleep."

Maria glanced at her watch. "You should go to bed now. Morning comes early around here."

Kayla covered a yawn. She agreed, it was bedtime. She looked at Boone, who was already heading for the door. The limp she'd noticed previously was more pronounced tonight.

"Get some sleep and try not to worry." He stopped just short of exiting.

She nodded. Of course she wouldn't worry. She was in a strange home with people she didn't know. And someone she didn't know wanted to harm her. What did she have to worry about?

"Stanford?"

She met the dark gaze of her protector.

He smiled that easy smile of his. "Don't worry."

Of course.

"If you need anything," Maria said, "don't hesitate, just ask."

They left and she was alone. What she truly needed, they couldn't give her. She didn't even know how to put a name on the empty spaces in her heart. For several years she'd filled those spaces up with anger, with rebellion and a lifestyle that had worn her out physically and emotionally.

She always wondered about the people who seemed emotionally whole and happy. How did they do it, find that happiness?

Alone she sat on the edge of the bed, her hands splayed on the cottony softness of the quilt. On the stand next to the bed was a Bible. It was small, leather bound and worn. Her gaze wandered from that small book to the needlepoint picture on the wall with a Bible verse she'd heard most of her life. "I can do all things through Christ who strengthens me."

The words were lovely and encouraging. But her heart still felt empty.

"She's a lovely girl," Boone's mom said as she followed him out to his truck. He opened the door of the old Ford and leaned against it.

"Mom, go ahead and say what you want to say. I need to get home and get some sleep."

"You need to get off your feet."

"Yeah, that, too." He took a seat behind the wheel of the truck, his hand on the key.

"Just be careful. She's pretty and lonely."

And there it was. He let out a long sigh. His mom knew him better than anyone. She also had a hard time remembering that her kids were growing up. "No need to worry. I'm going to do my job and then return her to her family."

"She doesn't have a family, not really."

He leaned back in the seat and closed his eyes. "Now I know where I get the fixer complex. From you. You're worried about me getting too involved." He opened his eyes and smiled at her. "But you know that you're just as bad."

She laughed. "I won't deny that. I look at this girl, and I see that she's lonely and hurting and could easily fall in love with her rescuer."

"I've been hired to do a job. I'll make sure all she feels for me is annoyance."

His mother patted his cheek and smiled. "You're so handsome, my son. And so clueless."

"Stop." He leaned and gave her a hug. "I'll see you in the morning."

He headed down the driveway to the RV. It always felt good to come home, even to his thirty-foot camper. The place was quiet. It had a front deck he'd built earlier in the spring. His dog was curled up on a patio chair, waiting for him. Yeah, home sweet home.

He limped up the steps and sat down on the chair next to the dog, propping his feet up on the footstool. Man, it felt good to stretch. He reached, rubbing the calf muscle of his right leg. The pain eased.

He let out a deep breath and relaxed again.

The collie that had been sleeping half crawled into his lap, resting her head on his leg. He brushed a hand down her neck. "Good girl."

She pushed at his hand with her nose.

"You're right, time to go inside."

He eased to his feet and headed inside. The door wasn't locked. It never was. He flipped on a light and headed for the kitchen. Halfway across the small living area, he stopped and took a step back.

"What in the world are you doing in my house?" he yelled at the man sprawled on his couch.

"Sleeping," Daron McKay grumbled. "And I could sleep a lot better without all the yelling. Did you get her settled?"

Daron tossed off the afghan and brushed a hand over his face as he sat up. Boone limped across the room and settled into the recliner.

"Yeah, my mom has her. And is already worried about feeding her. And keeping her safe from me. Or maybe me safe from her."

Daron perked up at that. "Your mom is a smart woman. We should hire her."

Boone tossed a pillow, hitting Daron in the head. "Go away."

"You're the one who told me the place is always unlocked."

"I didn't mean for you to move in here. You have a place of your own just down the road. A big place. Paid for by your dear old dad."

"It's too big and empty." Daron shrugged and plopped back down on the couch. "I'll pay for the food I eat and the inconvenience."

"I like to be alone."

"I know. It's easier to pace all night if there's no one watching."

They both did a lot of pacing. For different reasons. He gave his business partner a long look and wondered just how bad Daron's nights were. Since they usually stayed out of each other's heads, Boone could only guess. And since they dealt with their shared grief, their shared memories of Afghanistan, by being men and not dealing with it, he wasn't about to get all emotional now.

"My pacing is none of your business, McKay. We're business partners, not the Texas version of the *Odd Couple*."

Daron had stretched back out on the sofa and pulled the afghan up to his neck. "You can argue all you want, but you know you like my company. And if we're the *Odd Couple*, I'm the clean freak and you're the messy one. How is our client?"

"You're the slob. And she's scared. Even if she pretends she isn't. And probably lonely. I don't know." Boone stretched his legs, relieving the knots in his muscles. "There's something she isn't telling us."

"Charm it out of her."

"You're the charming one in this partnership. I'm all business. Luce is, well, Luce."

"She's only happy with a gun in her hand," Daron quipped.

It wasn't really the truth, but they liked to tease her.

"Yeah. So you charm Miss Stanford. I'll keep her safe."

"Nah," Daron said. "I think I'll let you try charming for once. I'm out on this one. She's a handful and I'm not patient."

"I was going to make a sandwich." Boone pushed himself out of his chair. "Want one?"

"I ate all of your lunch meat. Sorry."

"I'm changing my locks." Boone headed for the kitchen, where he rummaged through the cabinets, not finding much to choose from. He grabbed a can of pasta and decided to eat it cold, out of the can.

Daron joined him in the kitchen, his face haggard, his dark blond hair going in all directions and his shirt untucked. For the supposed neat one, he was a mess. Boone accepted that it was going to be a long night. He could feel it in his bones. Literally. He could feel it in the places where skin and muscle had been ripped, in the bones that had been broken. He could feel it in his mind. And that was the worst.

For the first time he was thankful for the distraction of Kayla Stanford. And even for Daron. If he had something to focus on, he'd concentrate less on the pain, on the memories.

But Kayla Stanford proved to be the wrong place to direct his thoughts. Because when he thought about her, what came to mind was the haunted expression she tried to cover up with a smile. The way her scent, something oriental and complex, lingered in the cab of his truck. He sniffed the sleeve of his shirt, because he could still smell her perfume.

Daron gave him a long look, eyes narrowed and one corner of his mouth hiked up. "What are you doing?"

"Nothing. I smelled something. Probably you." He made a show of smelling the canned pasta. "Maybe it's this?"

"You're losing it." Daron grabbed Boone's sleeve and inhaled. "And you smell like expensive perfume. Lucy doesn't wear perfume."

Boone couldn't help it, he took another whiff. When he did, his eyes closed of their own volition. He thought he would picture her teasing smile. Instead, he pictured the woman sitting in his truck trying to hide the tears that slid down her cheeks.

Yeah, it was going to be a long night. He had her scent clinging to his shirt and the memory of her tears. The two combined equaled disaster as far as he was concerned.

Chapter Four

Someone screamed and Kayla shot straight out of the bed, her heart racing and her legs shaking as she stood in the middle of the unfamiliar room. White curtains covered a window that revealed a view of fields that stretched to the horizon and the distant hills of Texas Hill Country. A cat was curled up at the foot of her bed. A cat?

She looked at the calico feline, white with black and orange patches, and wondered how it had gotten in here. The cat stretched and blinked, fixing green eyes on her, as if she were the interloper.

The scream echoed through the house a second time and she realized it was more of a shriek. Someone else shouted, then a door slammed. Obviously the entire family was up.

And if she hadn't been mistaken last night when Mrs. Wilder gave the list of names and locations of her children, there were several of them.

Although she was tempted to hide away in her room, Kayla dressed and brushed her hair. Before walking out the door of her borrowed bedroom, she glanced back at the cat.

"Don't you have mice to chase?"

The feline yawned, stretched and closed her eyes.

"I don't like cats," she said out loud. The cat didn't seem to care.

"I don't like them much myself. Did the screaming banshees downstairs wake you up?"

She spun to face a younger man, maybe in his early twenties. He had dark curly hair cut close to his head, snapping brown eyes, dimples and a big smile.

"I'm Jase." He held out a hand. "I'm the middle brother and also the smart one. No offense to your bodyguard."

She still hadn't spoken. He took her by surprise, with his easy banter and open smile. A few months ago she would have flirted. But she had given it up along with everything else.

For the past few months her goal had been a less complicated life.

This did not fit those plans.

"I would say 'cat got your tongue.'" He glanced past her to the cat in her room. "But that's pretty cliché."

"Um, I'm just…" She couldn't speak.

"Overwhelmed?"

"Maybe a little," she admitted.

"The cat's name is Sheba. As in queen of. She lives up to it. And she wouldn't chase a mouse if it crawled across her paws. Let me walk you downstairs. There's safety in numbers. And there's probably some breakfast in the kitchen. We usually eat after we've fed the livestock."

"You've already fed the livestock? What time is it?"

He laughed. "Just after seven. And yes, we've fed, pulled a calf and gathered eggs."

"Pulled a calf where?"

He gave her a sideways glance and grinned. "Pulled meaning delivered. The calf wasn't coming out on his own so we helped the mama with the delivery. There's nothing like starting your morning with a new life. Which I guess is why I'm premed."

While they'd been talking he'd led her

downstairs and through the house to the big country kitchen, where it seemed half the county had congregated for breakfast.

Boone's mom, Maria, was standing at the stove. Two young women who looked identical were setting the table. Another sister, a little older than them, was at the sink, auburn hair falling down to veil one side of her face. A toddler on pudgy legs, her curly blond hair in pigtails, was playing with bowls and wooden spoons.

"Welcome to our zoo," Jase Wilder said with a big smile that included everyone in the room. "The twinkies over there are Esmerelda and Alejandra. Better known to all as Essie and Allie, named after our grandmothers. They're not as identical as they like to pretend. In the kitchen is Mama Maria, whom you met last night. Michaela and her daughter, Molly. And my lovely sister Janie."

Janie with the auburn hair shot him a look and said nothing. Jase smiled back and answered, "Yeah, I know, Lucas is your favorite."

"Kayla, I hope we didn't wake you." Maria Wilder pointed at her twin daughters. "Those two can't keep quiet for anything."

The sister Janie half smiled her direction.

"They're excited because you're staying here. And you know all about fashion. They want to enter a twin pageant in San Antonio."

"Don't let them push you around," Michaela warned with a half tilt of her mouth. She appeared to be in her midtwenties and as she spoke she reached to pick up her little girl. "If you're going to survive, you have to stand your ground and become great friends with the word *no*."

Kayla would have answered but the conversation was interrupted by the sound of the front door closing and voices raised in discussion, and then Boone along with a younger man in his late teens, and possibly their father, entered the kitchen.

The older Wilder, gray haired and thin, pushed a walker. His steps were slow and steady. He glanced up at her and grinned. She saw the resemblance between him and his eldest son.

"I'm sorry I wasn't up to meet you last night," Jesse Wilder said as he made his way to the table. "But it looks as if you're surviving. It takes some backbone and sometimes selective hearing where this bunch is involved."

Boone, wearing dirt-stained jeans and a button-up shirt, winked as he headed for the kitchen sink. "If it takes backbone, I think she'll survive Clan Wilder with no problems."

She'd been surviving for a long time. It just hadn't always looked like it to the outside world.

"The mama cow didn't make it." Boone rinsed his hands, then splashed his face. Blindly he reached around, searching for a towel.

Kayla found one and pushed it into his hands. He dried his face and draped the towel over a cabinet door.

Jase's smile had slipped away. "I thought we had her up?"

"Yeah, I thought she was okay. About thirty minutes ago she went down and we couldn't get her back up."

"She was our best cow," Mr. Wilder said. He was pale, she noticed, and his hands trembled as reached for the cup of coffee Maria set down in front of him. He hooked his free arm around his wife.

"We'll make do, Jesse. We always have." She kissed the top of his head. "And I made a big breakfast."

"Because eating makes everything better," Essie, dark haired with flashing green eyes, quipped as she brought a plate of bacon to the table. "And coffee. That's the icing on the cake of life."

And they were all talking again, laughing and sharing smiles. Kayla stood to one side, watching, comparing this tumult with her family. The Stanfords, not the Martins. Her father's family was quiet, disciplined and perfect. Always perfect. She had never fit.

The Martins were more like this family. More open. More accepting. They relied on their faith and openly shared it with others. But they never pushed. She liked that about them.

She liked them. And yet she didn't feel as if she belonged. She wasn't a Martin. She wasn't a Stanford. She was the extra, the one who didn't fit.

Her gaze slid to Boone. He was still standing in the kitchen, his arm around the sister named Janie. Kayla felt a tightness in her own throat as she watched brother and sister. He spoke quietly. Janie responded. And then a hand moved and she brushed back that curtain of auburn hair, revealing a tight, puckered scar that ran from her cheek down her neck.

Someone stepped close to Kayla, and an arm brushed hers. "Don't stare. If you want a friend, she's the best, but she doesn't like pity."

"What happened?" Kayla asked.

"She was burned in an accident years ago." Jase shrugged as if what he said was common knowledge and not heartbreaking.

Conversation ended as the family all came to the table. Boone was suddenly at Kayla's side. He pointed to a chair and then he took the one next to it, his arm brushing hers. Before she could think, he had her hand in his. Michaela, next to her, took her other hand. The family bowed their heads in unison and Jesse Wilder prayed, thanking God for their food, for their blessings, for another day to serve Him.

After they all said amen, conversation erupted again. Kayla accepted a piece of bacon. Boone forked a pancake onto her plate, ignoring her protests that she really didn't eat breakfast. But he didn't speak to her. He laughed at a story his brother Lucas told. He shook his head at the twins when they told him they were going to try team roping.

There was much laughter and teasing as the family consumed the large breakfast. Kayla ate, not even realizing that she'd cleaned her plate. She felt as if she were in a foreign world here. Austin, just about an hour away, seemed as though it might as well be on a different planet.

When she'd discovered she had a bodyguard, she hadn't expected this. He should be in the background, quietly observing. Her father was a lawyer and a politician; she'd seen bodyguards and knew how they did their jobs. And yet here she sat with this family, her bodyguard talking of cattle and fixing fence as his sisters tried to cajole him into taking them to look at a pair of horses owned by Kayla's brother Jake Martin.

A hand settled on her back. She glanced at the man next to her, his dark eyes crinkled at the corners and his mouth quirked, revealing a dimple in his left cheek.

He opened his mouth as if to say something but a heavy knock on the front door interrupted. He pushed away from the table and gave them all an apologetic look.

"I think I'll get that." His gaze landed on Kayla. "You stay right where you are until I say otherwise."

"They wouldn't come here," she said. She'd meant to sound strong. Instead, it came out like a question.

"We don't know what *they* would or wouldn't do, because we don't know who *they* are. Stay." He walked away, Jase getting up and going after him.

Kayla avoided looking at the people who remained at the table. Conversation had of course ended. She knew they were looking at her. She knew that she had invaded their life.

And she knew that her bodyguard might seem like a relaxed cowboy, but he wasn't. He was the man standing between her and the unknown.

Boone stepped to the window before going to the front door. He moved the curtain and peeked out. Jase was behind him, of course. Little brothers could never mind their own business.

"I didn't ask for backup," Boone said as he let the curtain drop back into place.

"No, you didn't. But we're brothers."

"It's just Jake. He must have found out she's here."

Jase had the nerve to turn tail and run. "Have fun with that. I think it's my turn to do dishes."

"Dishes, my—" he watched his brother head down the hall "—foot."

He opened the door to Jake Martin. He didn't remember Jake being quite so tall, or so angry. Yeah, it made him pity Remington Jenkins more than ever. Remington had fallen hard for Samantha Martin ten years ago when the two had been teens. Jake had run him out of town.

Boone wasn't a seventeen-year-old kid, and he had a job that included keeping Kayla Stanford safe. So when faced with Jake's glowering look, he just smiled and leaned against the door as if all was well. Boone had learned long ago that silence always proved successful in getting the other person to talk.

"I want to know why my sister is here and not at our place, Wilder. I want to know why we weren't informed that she might be in danger."

Boone stepped onto the porch and closed the door behind him. Jake stepped out of his way. When Boone headed down the stairs and toward the barn, Jake followed.

"Is there a reason you won't answer me?" Jake continued as Boone opened the barn door.

"Because I don't answer to you. I answer to Kayla and her father." He felt bad about that, but he wouldn't break confidentiality clauses. "I *would* like to know how you found out she was here."

"She texted Samantha."

Boone spun around to face the other man, forgetting for a second that his balance wasn't always the best. He reached for the wall and steadied himself. "She did what?"

Jake gave him a tight smile. "What, you didn't know? She's not going to make this easy for you. And I don't appreciate not being kept in the loop."

"Then, we'll sit down together, the three of us, and she can tell you what you want to know. If she wants you to be told, that is. But I can't keep her safe if she's texting everyone in the state."

A throat cleared and he sighed. Kayla was standing in the doorway, early-morning sunlight streaming behind her, leaving her face in shadows.

"I'm not a child. You can do your job, Boone, but you're not going to keep me from my family."

Frustrated didn't begin to describe how he felt at that moment. "I wouldn't think of keeping you from your family. I would like to keep you safe. And I need honesty and a little cooperation from you to do that."

"Honesty?" She narrowed those magnificent blue eyes at him. "You want honesty?

I can do honesty. I honestly want to live my own life. I know I've messed up. I know they think they have something they can use against my dad. But I'd like for everyone to leave me alone. I was doing fine. I was getting my life together. I was finding pieces of myself I left behind. I was doing it. Alone. And I don't need..." She sobbed, the sound catching in her throat, and her eyes widened.

Jake shook his head. "Part of your problem, Kayla, is that you don't have to be alone. In any of this."

"Not right now, Jake." Boone knew when a woman was about to fall apart. Jake had never been soft or subtle. "Why don't you head home and we'll call you."

Boone left the older man standing there as he took Kayla by the hand and led her from the barn. She gripped his hand hard, clenching her fingers around his. He didn't really have a plan; he just knew if she was going to fall apart, the barn wasn't the place to do it. She didn't need to be where anyone could walk in. The last thing she needed was a lecture about family from an older brother who had just showed up in her life last year.

As they walked she seemed dazed, moving her feet one in front of the other without really paying attention. He kept hold of her hand, keeping her upright and moving. They ended up at his place. He led her up the steps and inside.

Thanks to Daron, the place smelled like wet dog, dirty socks and burned eggs. She wrinkled her nose but didn't say much. He pointed her toward the sofa and she complied without argument.

"Do you want something to drink?"

She laughed at the question. Boone brushed a hand across his face and shook his head.

"Iced tea?" he offered the second time around.

"Thank you." She sat curled up on his sofa, legs tucked beneath her. She reached for the afghan, sniffed and tossed it back to the opposite end. "You have a dog."

He laughed. "Yeah, I have a dog. And I have Daron McKay. Both of them shed, smell and leave messes."

What had started as laughter on her end suddenly turned into quiet sobs as he poured the tea. He grabbed two glasses and headed her way. She didn't cry pretty. Or maybe she didn't cry often and so this was the proverbial dam bursting. He sat down next to her, placing the glasses on the coffee table.

She didn't look like a woman who wanted a hug. She was stiff and curled into the corner of the sofa. He let her be because his sister Janie was like that. She wanted to do it all herself, alone, even grieve. He was his mother's son, so it was hard for him to let someone grieve alone. He wanted to wrap his arms around the person and he wanted to make it all okay.

Kayla elicited that response from him quicker than he would have imagined. She was about as broken as a woman could get, hiding all of that destruction behind her brazen actions and big smiles.

He wanted her pieced back together and whole.

Not that it should matter to him. She wouldn't be in his life that long. He guessed it was a little like his Scout leader used to say about a wilderness camping trip. Leave it better than you found it.

He'd like to leave Kayla a little better off when they parted ways.

Next to him, she'd stopped crying. She shifted, moving toward him by slow degrees. When her head touched his shoulder and she sighed, he came undone just a little. Expect the unexpected, that was what he knew about her. This softness would definitely qualify as unexpected. She melted against his side, her arm digging into his ribs just the slightest bit. He shifted and somehow that put her a little closer rather than putting distance between them.

Her face was in the crook of his neck, her breath warm, her touch light. And then she shifted a bit more, and her mouth touched his. This was crossing the line. He had that thought just as her hands moved to his shoulders, turning him to face her.

She brushed her lips over his, hesitant and seeking. The third time he fell into the kiss, giving up a little control. Her hand, soft and timid, was on his cheek. He pulled her a little closer and her hand slid to the back of his neck, her fingers skating through his hair.

Outside the dog barked; a truck door closed. He pulled away. She moved back, her eyes bright.

He started to apologize but she shook her head. "Please don't say you're sorry. Even if you are. I've felt empty for so long, Boone. I've raced through life trying to fill up the empty spaces. I've kissed men who meant nothing and made me feel nothing. You have no idea how much I needed that kiss. I needed to know that I could still feel."

What could he say to that? He sat back on the sofa and closed his eyes.

"I'm not sure I want to be your experiment, Kayla."

"I know. I'm sorry." She waited until he looked at her and then she grinned, a little mischievous and kind of sweet. "But it was a good kiss. I mean, if you're worried or have doubts, you shouldn't."

Boone grinned.

"I'll apologize now for the text to Samantha." Their shoulders were touching, her fingers laced through his.

"I don't mind if you call your sister. But we have to keep communications to a minimum so that it doesn't leak out that you're here. Family. No one else."

"Got it. Family. No one else."

The front door opened. Man, he'd forgotten all about that truck door a few minutes ago. He moved quickly, pulling his hand from hers. Kayla remained seated, as if nothing at all had happened.

Daron stepped into the camper, pulling off his hat, swiping a hand through his hair. He stopped when he saw the two of them.

"Oh, I didn't realize we had company." Daron stood in the center of the room looking from one to the other of them. "Kayla, it's been a while."

"Daron, I wish it had been longer."

Boone looked at them. "I have to agree with Kayla on this one. What are you doing back at my place?"

Daron shrugged and headed for the kitchen. "I skipped breakfast."

"I'm sure my mom has leftovers," Boone offered.

"No, thanks. I don't want to impose."

"You're imposing now. And shouldn't you be at the office?"

Daron pulled a container of juice out of the fridge and took a drink from the carton. He swiped a hand across his mouth and set the juice on the counter. "You know that our clients don't show up at the office. They call or email us. I've got one on the line right now for Lucy. I'll keep you posted on that."

"Good to know. Kayla and I were just heading out. We're going to visit her sister."

"That's good. Have you heard anything from the police today? I called her father. He hasn't had any threats in the past couple of days. He's been making a list of people who might dislike him enough to hurt him or his family. He'll give us a copy and the state police and FBI will get copies. I told him to think beyond the people who dislike him the most. Sometimes it's the least likely person. Someone only slightly offended but more than slightly deranged could be our man. Or woman."

"I think that narrows it down to almost everyone he knows," Kayla quipped.

Boone took hold of her arm and pulled her out the door with a parting shot at his partner. "I guess you plan on being here when I get back?"

Daron saluted as he opened the microwave. "Looks that way."

"Good, then we'll take shifts at my folks."

Daron grunted a response and Boone closed the door before he could form an objection.

"Why shifts?" Kayla asked as they headed toward his truck.

"I want to make sure one of us is watching you at all times."

"You shouldn't have to lose sleep," she insisted. "No one knows where I'm at."

"Let me do my job, Kayla. And you could help by not sending texts to anyone other than family."

"Right. I'm your job. I'm sorry."

Great. The kiss hadn't even been his idea,

and yet it still felt like his mistake. He guessed he could tell her the kiss hadn't left him empty, either. No, he wouldn't go there. Better to let sleeping dogs lie, and pretend kisses like that hadn't happened.

Chapter Five

Somehow they ended up with the twins, Essie and Allie, riding along to the Martin Ranch. And that meant switching to an extended-cab pickup. The girls climbed in the back. Kayla took the front passenger seat and tried to ignore the man behind the wheel. Which wasn't an easy thing to accomplish.

Because breathing meant noticing. When she inhaled, she caught his scent. He smelled good. He smelled of the outdoors, clean soap and spicy aftershave that reminded one of spruce trees and autumn. She turned her attention to the window and listening to the twins discuss a horse. Allie wanted to team rope. Essie was the aspiring model. They were compromising. Both would team rope. Both would enter the beauty pageant in San Antonio.

They were sisters the way she hoped she and Samantha would become sisters. They were on their way to that kind of relationship. Even if they were twenty-some years late to the game. This past summer they'd painted Sam's kitchen together. They'd been together when their mom had gasped her last breath and went on to whatever eternal reward might have been hers.

That death had hit them both hard in different ways. Sam had felt abandoned by their mother, Sylvia. Kayla had as well, but she'd been fortunate to have found her mom sooner. And for a short time she'd been the daughter, the one person in Sylvia Martin's life who knew her and loved her and felt loved by her.

With her passing, Kayla had been forced to take a long, hard look at her own life.

The rewind hadn't been pretty to view.

"Kayla, do you think emerald or ruby would be perfect for our gowns?" Essie asked from the backseat.

Kayla smiled back at the girls. "Either. Or maybe both. You don't have to match, do you?"

The girls looked at each other, eyes widening. "Perfect," they said in unison.

"Too easy," Boone grumbled. "Don't expect it to always be like that. They came out of the womb tugging hair and screaming at each other. Mom said if I'd shared a cramped space for nine months, I'd be a little testy, too."

The twins disagreed. "We love each other. We just have different opinions," Allie leaned forward to explain.

While the banter continued. Kayla's phone buzzed. She pulled it out of her pocket and read the text.

Poor little Kayla, her daddy didn't believe her and thought she was crying wolf. Maybe we should tell the world and then someone might believe you. Your bodyguard, for instance.

She went cold and her lungs wouldn't draw in a breath she desperately needed. The twins were still talking, although the conversation buzzed from far away. Boone said her name, not once but several times. She rolled down the window of the truck and threw the phone, watching in the rearview mirror as it bounced along the pavement of the country road.

"Oh, boy," one of the twins said in a low whisper. "So maybe just drop us off at Oregon's shop. We can get a ride home."

"Good idea," Boone said.

They got to town and he pulled onto the main street of Martin's Crossing. He parked in front of Oregon's. The sign in the window said it was open. The twins bailed out the back, quiet as mice.

"We're going back to get that phone."

"No." She shivered in the air-conditioned cab of the truck. "No, we're not."

"What was it, then?"

"I don't want to discuss it with you. It's a private matter between my father and myself."

"We need that phone. That's our only link to this guy. If he keeps telling us what he's thinking, we might be able to catch him. He might slip up eventually and give himself away."

"You're a bodyguard, not a cop."

"Honey, I was the toughest of cops. I've policed the world and hunted down terrorists. I promise you, I'm more than a bodyguard."

She shrank inside herself, wanting to be alone. She wanted to get away from him and the temptation to tell him all of her sorry secrets. Because he might believe her. He might. But what if he didn't? The little girl inside her still cried for someone to trust. And she didn't want to misplace that trust.

"We're going back for the phone," he insisted.

"Fine, go back."

"Tell me what happened." His voice had grown harder, more insistent.

"I can't. Just get the phone and tell my father that I didn't do this."

"You tell him. It seems to me that a little communication in this family of yours might be just the thing."

"Some parents don't want to communicate, Boone. Don't come at me with family advice when you live up on Walton's Mountain with homemade bread, church on Sundays and all of that encouragement."

He pulled to the side of the road where she'd thrown the phone. "I was wrong. You know how to communicate."

She closed her eyes. "I'm sorry. It isn't you that I'm angry with."

"No, I didn't think it was."

He said it so gently that her heart tugged at her, telling her to trust. She closed her eyes, trying to get a grip on that wild part of herself that wanted to outrun the pain, that wanted to push away anyone who tried to break through her defenses. She was so tired of fighting.

She was in over her head with this man who caused that shift in her emotions. What did the client develop with the bodyguard? Patients and caregivers developed the Nightingale syndrome. Captives developed Stock-holm syndrome. What did she have? The Kevin Costner syndrome. She smiled at the thought.

Handsome bodyguard, strong but wounded heroine. She laughed out loud. As he stepped out of the truck to retrieve her phone, he glanced back.

"You find this amusing?"

She shook her head. He was going to think she'd lost it.

"No, it isn't. I'm just trying to find humor in a really rotten situation."

He returned a minute later with her phone, and he tossed it to her as he got behind the wheel. "What's the big secret, Stanford? What didn't your dad believe?"

"You didn't have the right to read my texts," she told him.

"I do have the right. I thought this was just an easy gig, follow the heiress and keep her out of trouble. Instead, I'm fighting to keep you safe from a stalker, and from yourself. So if I have to read your texts in order to do my job, I will."

"Some things are private. Why do you limp?"

"Some things are private."

"What happened in Afghanistan, Wilder? Why do you live in a camper and not with your very awesome family? Why is Daron holing up in your place and not the big mansion his daddy bought so he could play rancher?"

"Watch those claws, Stanford." He pushed his white cowboy hat back a smidge on his head, giving her a better look into his dark brown eyes.

"I'm just saying, we all have secrets."

They sat there in the truck on the side of the road. "Let me tell you something about secrets. Secrets get people hurt. Or worse, killed. I'm trying to protect you, but I can't do that if you don't tell me what's going on."

"Could we please go now?"

He pulled onto the road.

"I can't do this, not yet." She needed time to be strong, and then she could tell him. Or tell someone. She knew it would come out. Sooner or later it was going to be revealed. If not by her, then by the blackmailers. How did they know?

"Okay. I'm not going to push." He pulled onto the road that led to the cottage where Samantha lived.

They drove past Duke and Oregon's house. The truck bounced and bumped along the rougher dirt portion of the road. In the distance she could see the roof of Brody and Grace's house. She shifted to look at the profile of the man behind the wheel of the truck. Boone Wilder. He'd been in her life only a week. She didn't owe him her story.

But she did wonder how it would feel to tell him, to have him listen and understand. How would it feel to have someone tell her they believed her?

"My dad and I are going to have to talk. We've been sweeping things under the rug for so long. And now it looks as if someone is going to force us to face this."

"Talk to him, then. Whatever it is, the power these blackmailers have over him is the secrecy and obviously the lack of trust between father and daughter. Take that advantage away from them and they fail."

"You make it sound easy."

"Tell Samantha. She can help you." He pulled the truck up behind her sister's truck.

Sam waved from the arena where she was working her barrel horse. She'd tried to teach Kayla to ride. It had not been a great experience. But she thought she might like to try again. Because riding meant trusting.

If she could trust a thousand-pound animal,

maybe she could trust her father. She could trust Boone. She could trust her heart.

Boone watched from a distance as the sisters talked. They were full of smiles and hugs. Then they walked together, the horse trailing behind them. From a distance he saw Kayla run her hand down the neck of the horse. He smiled. Maybe he'd give her riding lessons. That would be a way to pass some time.

His phone rang. He pulled it out of his pocket and he wasn't surprised that the call was from Kayla's father. He answered.

"Did my daughter get a text?"

Hello to you, too. Boone grinned at his own humor. "Yes, sir, she did. She isn't in the mood to talk about you or to you. I think that's a mistake. These blackmailers know your secrets. Or at least they think they do. I know the goal is to catch them and put a stop to this. But as long as you're keeping your secrets, they have all the power."

A deadly silence hung between them for a long minute.

"Don't tell me about power, Mr. Wilder. I know all about power. And don't tell me what I already know about my daughter." There was a break in either the connection or the other man's voice.

"I'm just saying..." Boone began. But then he didn't know how to continue. Everything sounded like an accusation, and that wasn't a bodyguard's place.

He glanced in the direction of the corral, where the sisters were talking. This simple babysitting job was taking on levels he hadn't expected, and didn't want.

"I'm going to hunt these men down," Mr. Stanford was saying. "I'm going to make them pay."

"It sounds as if you might want to deal with a few other things first. What is it you didn't believe?"

Mr. Stanford said a few choice words followed by, "Do your job, Wilder. You were hired to be a bodyguard, not a family counselor."

Boone brushed a hand through his hair and let out a long breath. "I'm sorry, that was uncalled-for."

"You bet it was. If you don't want to lose this job, remember who is paying your salary."

Boone nodded and kept the phone to his ear. Because the salary was important to him. As much as he didn't want the money to be important, for his family and for the Wilder ranch, it was. They had medical bills to pay and kids to put through college. His career was the only thing between them and financial ruin.

"I'm protecting your daughter. I'll leave it to you to find the people threatening her life."

"I expect you to keep Kayla safe, out of trouble, and get her to my town hall meeting in San Antonio this Friday."

"We'll be there."

The call ended. Boone shoved the phone into his pocket and headed for the corral and the horse that Kayla was climbing on top of. Keeping her safe meant keeping her from falling off that crazy animal of Sam's. The horse was sidestepping, aware of the novice crawling on his back as if she was hanging on to a high wire and about to fall.

"Stanford, sit up straight and take a deep breath." He spoke quietly for fear of startling the already antsy animal. The horse hopped a little. "Sam, you have more sense than this."

Samantha, blonde, proud and unwilling to back down, arched a brow at his comment. "I know what I'm doing, Wilder."

"Of course you do. You're going to get her thrown."

"Thrown?" Kayla asked with not a hint of fear. No, instead she seemed to take his comment as a challenge. She took the deep breath and visibly relaxed. "I'm not going to get thrown. I'll have you know, I've been riding since I was twenty-four."

Both sisters laughed. He didn't.

"Fine, cowgirl, go on." He made a shooing motion with his hands. "Show us how it's done."

"The horse is tired. He'd prefer to just stand here. But thank you."

Boone took the reins from Sam, eased Kayla's left foot out of the stirrup and replaced it with his. Deep breath, he reminded himself. And then he was in the saddle behind her. The horse took off.

"Move your other foot," he told her.

She did and he slid his right foot into that stirrup. His arms were around Kayla and he wrapped her hands around the reins.

"What are you doing?" She sat poker stiff in front of him, bouncing like mad in the saddle as the horse trotted around the arena.

"Stop bouncing as if you're on a pogo stick. It's a horse. There's a beat, a rhythm. Hold the reins easy, not tight, not loose. Got it?"

"No, I don't *got* it. I don't ride, Wilder. I'm

a city girl. Remember? I shop. I go out to dinner. Green Acres is not the place for me."

He leaned into her back and for some crazy reason brushed his lips across her ear. "Smell the country air. Feel the horse moving beneath you. Green Acres is the place to be. Farm living is the life for me."

She laughed a little and he felt her relax. He guided her hand, showing her that she didn't have to pull the reins, just let them brush the horse's neck and the animal would turn away from the pressure. A light touch of the reins against the left side of the neck and the horse turned right. She rode him toward the first barrel and eased him around it.

He could feel the tension evaporating from her body. She was letting go. She was trusting the horse.

"Your sister is giving us the stink eye," he warned.

"Of course she is." Kayla reined the horse to the right and headed for the gate.

"You're a pro already." Boone let his hands settle on his legs. "It's as if you've been riding since you were twenty-four."

She glanced back over her shoulder, her smile sweet, her eyes flashing amusement. She kissed his cheek. It was a quick brush of her lips, like a butterfly landing but then moving on. But he felt it.

All the way to his heart.

Chapter Six

"I'd rather be anywhere other than at a town hall meeting listening to my father tell people he is going to make things better for a community." Kayla placed a hand on Boone's arm as he guided her down the steps of the Wilder home. He cleaned up well.

She wasn't about to tell him that, though. In the past week she'd come to the conclusion that her Kevin Costner syndrome might be more than her imagination. It was easy to be attracted to a handsome bodyguard, especially when he was a gentleman.

What she had to do, quite often, was remind herself that he was being paid to care about her. There might be a connection between them, but it would soon end. He would get a sizable check from her father. Then they would go their separate ways. He would stay on this ranch, raising cattle and training horses, and maybe someday he'd marry and have little Wilders. She would go back to... She didn't know what she'd go back to.

"Will you always do this, Boone?" she asked as he helped her into the black SUV, Lucy driving again.

He climbed in next to her. "Do what?"

"Ranch? Be a bodyguard?"

He removed his black cowboy hat and placed it on the seat between them.

"I guess I'll always be a rancher," he answered.

Lucy cleared her throat but didn't comment.

"What about you, Stanford? What are you going to do with your life when this is all over with?" Boone asked as the SUV got on the highway, headed in the direction of San Antonio.

What *was* she going to do with her life? She had thought more about that recently than she had in years. Being the thorn in her father's side no longer appealed to her. It had worn her down, pushed her to do things she couldn't undo and woke her up at night feeling a lot of regret.

"I have a degree in early childhood education," she admitted. "Once upon a time, I was a little girl who dreamed of being a teacher."

"Maybe you should pursue that dream," Lucy chimed in, no longer the silent observer. "I mean, it would be easier, wouldn't it?"

Kayla watched the landscape of Texas Hill Country fly past her from the tinted window of the SUV. Autumn wildflowers dotted the landscape, as did an occasional farm or aging barn. The patchwork of the countryside, greens, autumn browns, was dotted by the occasional small town. She had seen the sky view from a plane and that was what it always reminded her of, the patchwork quilts Grammy Stanford had loved so much. She wondered what had happened to those quilts.

"Still with us, Stanford?"

"Lost in the countryside," she answered. "Teaching. I don't know if I'd be a good teacher."

"Never know until you try."

"True. I never thought I'd like a cowboy," she teased.

He laughed. "And do you?"

A choking sound came from the front seat and Lucy glanced back. "Don't encourage him."

"I won't. I wasn't speaking of any particular

cowboy, Boone. My brothers are ranchers and cowboys. I am a little bit attached to them."

"There's hope for you yet, Stanford." He said it with an easy cowboy grin and a sparkle of mischief in his eyes.

It was easier when he called her Stanford.

The traffic got heavier as they drew closer to San Antonio. There were more houses, more businesses, more people. Her heart got heavier, too.

"Don't worry, we're with you," Boone said about thirty minutes from their destination, a hotel near the River Walk.

"I'm not worried. I've done so many of these events in my life, I'm used to being under the microscope."

He adjusted his tie. "I'm glad you're used to it."

She reached to fix his tie. "You've gotten it all crooked. Leave it. Or take it off. You look fine without it." She loosened the tie to pull it over his head. He looked fine in jeans, boots and a button-up shirt with a sport coat. He'd draped the coat over the back of the front passenger seat, but she'd seen it on him back at the Wilder ranch.

"Do I look fine, Stanford?" he asked with a wink.

"I told you not to encourage him," Lucy warned.

Kayla didn't answer. Soon she'd have to leave the safety of this SUV and brave her father's world. She wished she could face that world with something more than the false bravado she cloaked herself in. She longed to make eye contact with her dad and have him give her a look of encouragement. Or even love.

It seemed as if they'd been strangers for her entire life, but it had really been only in the past dozen years that things had fallen apart. Before that, she had been his little girl, going to work with him, sitting on his lap before bedtime. He'd been a good dad to a little girl who had been left on his doorstep by a woman who wasn't capable of living in the real world.

He'd married Marietta when Kayla was five. They'd gone from the two of them, father and daughter to a family of three. And soon after, Andrew came along. And then Michael. Not that she pictured herself as Cinderella. She had never thought of herself as the tragic fairy-tale heroine. Marietta hadn't banished her to the attic or forced her to do hard labor. She just hadn't wanted to raise someone else's child.

But she wasn't a terrible person. Kayla wondered how things would have been different if she'd told her stepmother what had happened and not her father ten years ago.

"We're here," Lucy informed them as they turned onto a side street, then pulled into a crowded parking lot. "And I'm only warning you once, Kayla, no stunts like the last time."

"Thanks for the warning."

"Okay, ladies, let's be friends." Boone opened his door and took a quick look around the area, then he reached for Kayla's hand.

A few minutes later they were inside the hotel and being directed to the conference room her dad had rented for the occasion. She found the term *town hall* amusing. Shouldn't it be in a town, held in a hall of some type and not in a luxury hotel, so that only certain people could attend?

"You know, he wasn't always this way, my father." She stood next to Boone as they waited for the elevator. He focused briefly on her and then past her.

"No?"

"Stop looking around as if you're afraid

someone will jump out of a potted palm," she told him.

"I'm sorry, but I'm afraid of palms. And I'm trying to keep you safe. So your father hasn't always been like this?"

"No. A long time ago he cared about the people who came to him as clients. He would tell me about them, about their troubles, their lives, and how he wanted to make things better for those people who trusted him."

"What happened?"

She had to glance away from him, from dark eyes that saw too deeply. "Money. Power. A business partner who didn't have the same moral compass."

"Paul Whitman?"

She shuddered at the mention of the name. "Yes, him."

"Met him. I wasn't impressed."

The elevator opened and they stepped on. As the doors closed, another man rushed to jump on. Kayla slid a little closer to Boone and felt his strong hand on her back. He looked down at her and one side of his mouth tilted. He was all confidence.

"Afraid of elevators?" he asked as they went up five floors.

"Only sometimes." She gave the man standing in front of them a pointed look.

"This one seems to be safe. Look, it even has an inspection sticker. And besides, what do you have to fear when I'm with you?"

"Nothing, of course." She meant it, she realized.

The other man got off the elevator on the sixth floor. Without a backward glance he was gone. Kayla let out a sigh.

"I don't want to live my life like this."

"I know you don't," Boone said, pausing as if he meant to say more.

"What?"

"You have choices. This will end soon, and then you can find out what you do want from your life."

"Easy words."

The elevator stopped at the eighth floor. He led her off the elevator, cautiously looking both ways before he put a hand on her arm and guided her in the direction of the conference room.

"It isn't going to go on forever." He spoke quietly as they neared the room from which they could hear the steady hum of conversations.

"I know."

Her phone chimed. She pulled it out of her purse. She would have hid it from Boone, but he was there, leaning over her shoulder. The screen of the phone was still shattered. But the words of the text were clear.

Your dad had his chance. Tomorrow's paper should be interesting.

"It looks as if he's upping his game," Boone said as he took the phone from her trembling hands. "Let's find your father."

"I should go. I should just leave and make this campaign easy for him."

Boone led her into the conference room and through the dozens of people. He seemed relaxed, and she realized that was his persona. Good-natured cowboy. But she saw the clench of his jaw, the way he constantly searched the crowd for danger. Danger. Someone wanting to hurt her. She'd lived her life laughing at circumstances, pushing the limits. She'd never thought of danger. Not like this. Never had a person want to harm her or destroy her father.

She edged closer to her bodyguard, thankful now that he was in her life, that her dad had known this would be necessary.

"There he is. And from the way he's looking at his phone, you're not the only one being texted." There was a hard edge to Boone's voice. It sent a chill up her spine.

This man knew how to protect.

"Get her out of here," her dad said quietly, moving them away from the crowd as they reached his side.

"I'd already made that decision. But I want to make sure you have a security detail of your own and a plan for whatever is going to be released to the paper tomorrow."

"Of course I don't have a plan." Kayla's father swiped a hand over his short, graying hair. "No one has a plan for blackmail, Wilder. And yes, I have a team of people. I don't need your help in this. I need to know that you're keeping my daughter safe."

And then Kayla's father looked at her. His eyes softened. "I never wanted to see you hurt this way. I don't even know what went wrong."

"Dad, you do. But this isn't the place to talk about that."

He paled and his gaze shifted to look past her. "God help us. Kayla, someone knows."

She fought the sting of tears and the emotions that tightened in her throat. She wanted him to believe her. She wanted him to be her father again and protect her. The past came back, all of the pain, the anger, the betrayal. Because she saw that look in his eyes all over again and she didn't know if he'd ever truly believed her.

"Knows what?" Boone's voice slid through the haze of pain.

"This doesn't concern you, Wilder. Just take care of my daughter."

"Yes, Boone, you take care of his daughter. He can't. He doesn't have time. He doesn't have the courage." She turned and walked away, ignoring her father, ignoring Boone as he called out to her to wait for him.

Pain waits for no man.

"Go with her," William Stanford ordered as Boone paused for a moment, waiting for more answers.

Boone shot him a look that he knew wouldn't quell the man or put him in his place. "Sir, I don't have a daughter, but I wonder if maybe you should be the one going after her."

"I have a job to do here, Wilder."

"You have a daughter walking out that door, and I think she's your responsibility."

"I'm paying you—"

Boone cut him off. "Yeah, a lot of money to do that for you. I get it. I'll go after her."

He hurried after Kayla, who had almost reached the door. As he ran, he tried to come up with a plan, because there was a lot going on that he didn't have answers to.

"Wait," he called out as she went through the door and headed left instead of right, toward the elevator.

She paused but didn't look back. She stood still, her shoulders straight and her head high. He walked up behind her but didn't touch her. Instead, he let out a sigh and waited. She needed a lot more than him.

He called Lucy. "We're heading down. No need for you to come up. We're going back to base."

"I don't want to go," she finally spoke. She wasn't crying.

"What do you want to do?"

She shrugged, her back still to him. He kept his distance, giving her space. "I don't really know. Six months ago I would have hopped a plane somewhere. Or I would have done my best to embarrass my father and make him pay. Now I don't know."

"Come on, we'll go home. Mom will make you some of her famous hot cocoa, and maybe she still has some of that banana bread."

"Hot cocoa would be nice," she whispered.

"Yeah, she'll ply you with cocoa and you'll feel as if she's the best friend you've ever had. I think you could use that friendship tonight, Stanford."

She nodded, acknowledging without admitting. She turned to face him, no tears, just stark pain, the kind that made him feel it in his own heart. Pain and betrayal.

They left the hotel in silence, made the ride all the way back to Martin's Crossing in the same way. Lucy would occasionally give him a questioning look in the rearview mirror. He could only shrug because he didn't have answers, only questions and maybe suspicions.

He tried to think of a scenario when his own dad wouldn't move heaven and earth to be there for his daughters, for all of his children. He tried to think how it would have felt if he'd been in that bed in an army hospital and he hadn't woken up to find his dad sitting next to him.

When they pulled up to the Wilder Ranch, the house looked half-asleep. It was barely ten o'clock but the Wilders believed in early to bed and early to rise. He opened the SUV's door and stepped out, giving Kayla room to exit the vehicle without touching him, which seemed to be her wish. As she walked toward the house, he waited, leaning against the driver's door. Lucy had opened the window.

"Well?" she asked.

"Another text. Something to be revealed in the morning paper. I think it's a serious bombshell. Father and daughter were at odds and she seemed to need something from him."

"Fathers aren't superhuman. They let their children down sometimes, Boone. You're spoiled. Your father is one of the best."

"I know, Luce. I'm sorry."

She raised a hand. "This isn't about me. She's a mess and I think we're in over our heads."

"Why do you think that?"

"Because she doesn't need a bodyguard. You know it and I know it. They need a family therapist and a good private investigator."

"You're probably right," he agreed.

She gave a roll of her expressive dark eyes. "I'm always right."

"Do you want to stay here tonight?" he offered.

"Nah, I'll be fine. Mama is determined to take those bulls to that buck out in Arkansas. I'm going to help her load in the morning."

"She's a strong woman, your mom."

"Yeah, she's my hero." She restarted the

SUV. "Boone." She paused and he looked back. "Watch yourself."

She touched her heart and then she shifted into Reverse and left. Great, just what he needed was Lucy all emotional and compassionate. He'd have to tell her tomorrow that he didn't need her to get all girlie on him. That would get her back on track.

Kayla had gone inside. He followed, finding her in the kitchen with his mom, the way he'd known she would be. He watched as the two of them mixed ingredients for Mexican hot chocolate. It wasn't even heating yet but he could smell the vanilla and the touch of cinnamon. Or maybe it was his imagination. He joined them at the stove, taking the place next to his mom and not Kayla.

"Make yourself a bed on the sofa, son." His mom patted his cheek. "You look tired."

"I'm good."

Her brows arched. "Of course you are. You're like your father, always good. Even when you aren't."

"Is Dad okay?"

She stirred the cocoa and the water that would help ingredients dissolve. "He says he is, of course. But I saw him today rubbing his chest. I worry."

He kissed the top of her head. "Of course you do. I'll see if I can't get him to go to the doctor Monday."

"Thank you," she spoke softly. "And you, my son. You've been going nonstop. You're limping. Take care of yourself, yes?"

"Yes," he agreed.

Kayla had sent brief glances his way as he and his mother talked to each other. He saw a hunger in her blue eyes. He knew that a moment like this was what she needed. His mom would give it to her, in spades. He'd do the guarding. His mom would do the heart work. It worked best that way. It kept him sharp and focused on the job he needed to do.

Time to make his escape. "I'll have a cup of that cocoa and then I'll leave the two of you alone. Girl talk is not my thing."

"No, you're more about the conformation of a good horse and which cows drop the best calves," his mom teased.

"A man has his priorities."

"I'll bring you a cup of cocoa. There are sheets and blankets in the hall closet."

That was his mom's way of dismissing him. He took the out she offered and left the two of them alone. The idea of getting off his feet made it easier to agree.

It didn't take him long to make up a temporary bed on the sofa. His sister's crazy cat, Sheba, appeared at his side. She gave him a long, unblinking look, then focused on his bed. Without an invitation she stretched, and then leaped. She curled up on the pillow and looked for all the world as if she thought it belonged to her.

"I don't think so, cat."

She exposed her belly for him to pet. He obliged and then moved her to the end of the sofa to a throw pillow that must have been placed there for her. She curled up on it and seemed perfectly content.

Boone raised his left pant leg, rubbed the aching muscles until they relaxed, and then he unhooked the prosthetic leg. He placed it on the floor under the coffee table. It was computerized, a complex thing that adjusted to his gait. He didn't want it stepped on or broken.

He rubbed his leg and stretched, and then he grabbed a pin off the table and rolled up the leg of his jeans to secure it.

"Boone?"

He looked up. "Stanford."

He looked down at his leg and then back to the woman standing in the center of the living room, a cup of cocoa in a hand that trembled. She was going to spill it on his mom's new carpet.

"Don't spill that," he said quietly, bringing her back to earth.

She managed to get the cocoa to him without spilling it. "I didn't know."

"You didn't need to know."

"Of course." She sat next to him. The room was dark except for the soft glow of the porch light through the window. The cat's purring broke the silence. It felt too intimate but he didn't know how to say it without drawing attention to the fact.

"Afghanistan?" she asked, bringing the subject back to his leg.

"Yeah, Afghanistan."

Silence again, other than the purring of Sheba.

"So we all have secrets," she finally said.

"Some secrets are dangerous. Some are just nonissues. This happened a few years ago. It's just a part of my life now, and unless the skin breaks down, I'm good. I don't classify it as a secret."

"My secrets, my life…" She broke off, shaking her head.

"You don't have to tell me your secrets,

Kayla. It isn't necessary. Unless you want to. And if you talk, I'll listen."

She grabbed the hot chocolate from his hands and took a sip, then she held the cup. He'd meant for her to share hot chocolate and secrets with his mom. Maybe he should remind her of that fact. His mom was the listener. He was the bodyguard.

"My dad's campaign adviser has been his law partner for years."

"Mr. Whitman."

"Yes."

"I see." He retrieved the chocolate from her and took a drink but he gave it back when she reached for it.

His mom appeared in the doorway of the living room. She stood for a moment watching the two of them and then disappeared again, leaving him to be the one who listened to secrets. He had a feeling the secrets were going to make him want to hurt someone.

They sat in silence a long time. At some point she set the cup down and reached for his hand, lacing her fingers through his. Upstairs someone was watching a late-night show, and the sound of audience laughter carried. Sheba continued to purr. And in the kitchen he could hear his mom washing dishes and the radio playing gospel music. She loved her alone time at night.

"My dad didn't believe me." The words were whispered but they sounded loud in the quiet of that room. Her fingers tightened on his and she leaned a little in his direction. "He was my dad. I trusted him. He should have trusted me. Instead, he told me he couldn't believe I'd make up something like that about a man who would do anything for me."

She laughed a humorless laugh. "Do anything for me. Which is funny, because Paul Whitman made me promise not to tell, but before that he'd promised he'd do anything for me. And if I told, he'd make sure no one ever believed me again."

"Someone should have believed you," Boone said as she tried to pull her hand from his. But he couldn't let her go. He couldn't let her run. "I believe you."

"Yes," she whispered on a broken sob. "Someone should have."

She pulled free from his hand and he let her go, let her curl up inside herself on the corner of the sofa, the cat pulled close for comfort. And this was why Kayla Stanford fought everything and everyone. She was broken and trying to trick the world into thinking she was whole.

He reached for her but she shrank from his touch. He picked up the blanket he'd left folded on a nearby footstool, covered her and stood. He balanced next to her, looking down at a woman who appeared confident but was hiding a hurting kid deep inside. The girl who had needed her father's protection was still seeking that security from him.

"I'll do whatever I can to help you," he promised, knowing he shouldn't. "But right now, I'll get my mom. She's not going to leave you alone tonight."

She nodded, brushing hair back from her face. "Boone, thank you."

"You're welcome."

He made his way from the room, hopping on a right leg that had adjusted and gotten stronger over the past few years. He made it to the kitchen and his mom gave him a look.

"Crutches, Boone."

"Too much trouble. You're needed in the living room. I think I should go and leave the two of you alone. But I'll apologize now for the long night you're going to have."

"Don't apologize. You see, when someone

is hurting they are like a sore. It can only hold the pain so long and then it's going to erupt."

"I'm not sure if that's the most beautiful way of putting it, Mom, but I guess it's accurate."

She shrugged and handed him a plate of banana bread. "Eat something. Kayla will be fine here. Don't try to go home like that. Crutches, son."

He kissed her cheek. "You're the best."

She smiled up at him. "And you are a good son. You have a good heart."

"My heart is intact, don't worry."

She picked up another plate. "So you say. But you know, someday your heart is going to…"

"Good night, Mom." He headed for the closet in the utility room. "Crutches in here?"

"Yes, they are. I'm only saying…" she started again.

"Mom, this isn't the time. You can trust me to know my own heart. I'm happy with my life the way it is right now."

"You're not getting any younger." The words followed him out the back door. "Hey, you left a leg in my living room."

"I'll get it tomorrow."

He would never call himself a chicken, or

even a coward, for running. He would call himself wise. He would call leaving at that moment self-preservation. Because his mom had two sides. The side that wanted to protect her son and the side that thought he would be happiest if he married and gave her grandchildren.

And he knew that Kayla needed more tonight than he could give. She needed to be held. She needed to cry. She needed to hear from a woman who had survived that she would survive.

No, he would never call himself a coward. He was the guy who would be sleeping in his truck, making sure no one set foot on this property and that no one hurt her again.

Not even him.

Chapter Seven

Kayla managed a few hours of sleep after a lot of crying and a lot of talking with Maria Wilder. It had felt good. For the first time in ten years someone had listened and believed her. She'd told Boone's mom about being a little lost in her early teens. Her dad had been busy with his career. Her stepmother had been busy being his wife and a mother to her two boys. She hadn't signed on to raise his daughter. There had been nannies for that. But nannies weren't mothers. They didn't explain what a girl growing into a woman needed to know. And they didn't take the place of a father who was suddenly too busy.

Kayla had been a victim in the making, the girl no one was really paying attention to. And Paul Whitman had known. He'd watched her drifting from her family. He'd offered rides home from school, a movie. He'd offered her time. He'd taken advantage and left her with no one to turn to.

She was the victim. At some point during the night, Maria Wilder had finally convinced her of that fact. And for the first time in years she felt the pieces fitting together again. Not whole, but closer than she'd been in a long time.

She sat up and looked out the window. Boone's truck was parked in the drive. She leaned over the sofa, and saw the prosthetic leg he'd left behind. It was an amazing piece of equipment, even attached to the leather cowboy boot. He would need it this morning.

She slipped her feet into her shoes and then grabbed the blanket, slipping it around her shoulders before she headed out the front door. Boone's dog, Sally, was sitting at the edge of the porch. The collie followed her down the steps and across the yard.

When she got to the truck, she tapped the boot against the window. He woke up with a start, reaching for something in his glove box. And then he saw her. He slid a hand across his face, rubbing the shadow of whiskers that had grown overnight.

He was beautiful, she thought. He was more than a handsome cowboy with dark eyes and dark hair, his skin bronzed from a life in the sun. No, he was more than that. Because of the kindness that settled in his eyes and the roguish smile that sometimes caught her by surprise.

But he was temporary. Yet this temporary stop in his life might have changed her life. Maybe that had been God's plan all along.

"You have my leg," he mumbled through the closed window of the truck. She opened the door.

"I thought you might want this." She handed it over.

"Yeah, I might. Did you get any sleep?" he asked.

"A little. No one else is up."

"It's Saturday. They might sleep in a little. Want to help me start breakfast?"

She glanced from him to the house. "Yeah, sure."

He pushed the door a little wider and hopped down from the truck. She glanced down, surprised that again she couldn't tell he wore the prosthetic.

"Amazing, isn't it?" he asked, lifting one leg and then the other.

"Very."

"And you have questions?"

Of course she did. "How did it happen?"

He tugged the blanket up around her shoulders. "That's a long story."

"It's none of my business."

"No, it's okay. It's just that it was another time, definitely another place and maybe another me. Daron and I wanted to help a family. A mother, a little brother, a sister."

She heard the catch in his voice and she touched his arm. He stopped walking and looked down at her. "Boone, I'm sorry."

He continued walking. "Me, too. The boy approached us one day and told us there were men in his mother's house and he was worried. I don't know, maybe he was telling the truth and he was afraid or maybe it was all a setup. I'll never know because the IED went off as a group of us headed that way to see if we could help. One of our guys died in that explosion. He left a pregnant wife behind. His little girl is three now."

"You didn't hurt them."

"No, I didn't. But I could have been more perceptive, could have been more focused. We'd gotten too relaxed, maybe. I don't know."

He led her through the house to the kitchen.

Jase was already up. He was starting a pot of coffee and eating a snack cake.

"Hey, didn't realize there was anyone else up," he said.

"I was in my truck. Kayla was on the sofa." Boone grabbed a carton of eggs out of the fridge. "I'm going to make scrambled eggs, toast and bacon. You eating with us this morning, Doc? Or was that chocolate cake it for you?"

"Yeah, I'm eating if you're cooking. Does Kayla cook?"

She laughed at that. "No, Kayla has never cooked."

"Then, Kayla should learn," Boone quipped. "Today is the first day of the rest of your life."

"Dramatic," Kayla informed him. "But I will learn to cook. After all, someday I'm going to be on my own. No one will be around to fix me omelets or biscuits and gravy."

Boone shot her a look as he pulled a big bowl out of the cabinet. "Going to be a teacher, are you?"

She managed a smile. "Yeah, I think I will be."

"Good for you," Jase said as he tossed her a snack cake.

"Drop the cake." Boone pushed the bowl

and the eggs in front of her. "Get busy, Stanford, you have a lot to learn."

"I know how to crack an egg."

"Yeah, but can you get it in the bowl without the shells?"

She shrugged. "I guess we'll find out."

Boone left her to it and he started the bacon frying. Jase pulled up a stool and watched. She cracked an egg on the counter and pulled it apart over the bowl. Of course part of the shell fell in. Jase didn't say a word. He just handed her a fork and took another sip of his coffee. She gave him a warning look when it seemed he might change his mind and say something.

After a few tries she got the hang of it and managed to hand over a bowl of eggs, sans shells. She gave Boone a smug look. He handed the bowl back to her.

"Whip them up with the fork and add some milk," he ordered.

"I thought that was your job."

He shook his head. "Nope, you're making the eggs. Someday you might have a classroom of hungry kids. What are you going to feed them?"

"Schools have cafeterias, Wilder."

He just went back to his bacon. She gave

Jase a pleading look. While Boone's back was turned, Jase took the bowl and the fork and whipped the eggs. She got the milk from the fridge and Jase added the right amount and handed the jug back to her.

He didn't even turn around. "Jase, let her do it."

"Eyes in the back of his head," Jase grumbled as he handed her the fork and pushed the bowl of eggs in her direction.

Kayla managed a shaky laugh. She hadn't expected to laugh this morning. Not today, when her life might become a newspaper headline. Not today, when that same story could destroy her father's career. She cared about that more than she'd expected to. She didn't want him hurt. As much as she'd tried to hurt him with her actions over the past few years, she didn't want this to be the thing that ended his career.

"Hanging in there, Stanford?" Boone took the bowl of eggs from her.

She watched as he poured them into a skillet. "Yeah, I'm good. I guess there isn't going to be an Austin morning paper around here?"

He laughed, a husky sound that shouldn't have sent shivers down her spine. "No paper here. But we'll take a look at the internet."

"Want me to get my computer?" Jase offered, already off the stool.

"That would work." Boone waited for his brother to leave the room and then he faced her again. "So you're really okay?"

"I woke up this morning feeling like a new person. Or maybe a person with faith. I expected that to get me through the day, but it isn't going to be that easy, is it?"

He opened his arms, a startling invitation that she found she couldn't refuse. His arms, strong and comforting on a morning when she was starting what appeared to be a new life but with the old life still needing to be dealt with. She stepped into the circle of his embrace and he pulled her close. It was a brotherly, comforting hug, but it included his strength, his scent, his warmth. Before he let her go he kissed her near her temple. She drew in a breath at the gesture, so sweet.

"You're dangerous, Wilder."

"No, ma'am, I'm about as dangerous as a newborn puppy."

She laughed at that. "Yes, exactly. Everyone wants a puppy."

Jase returned with the computer, giving them each a careful look, shaking his head as he sat back down. He opened the laptop and fired it up. "Looking for anything special?"

"Yes, and private." Boone took the computer and did a quick search as she looked over his shoulder.

The story was front page in the politics section. There was a picture of her at a party, wild-eyed, unfocused. The headline said Poor Little Party Girl.

"They did it."

"Yeah, they did. But let's read it all and see what we're dealing with." He spoke quietly, his arm coming around her, pulling her to his side. Together they read the article that told of secrets and a father who turned his back on his daughter.

"They didn't give up the whole story," Boone spoke quietly. As though he thought a loud voice might shatter her. It wouldn't, though. "They're holding on to the rest. It's their ace. They've got your dad's attention and now they'll set the hook and reel him in."

"I need to call him. I need for him to know that I wouldn't have done this to him."

Boone turned her to face him. "He needs to call you and tell you that he should have been there for you. He should have believed you. He's not the victim, Kayla. Don't treat him like one."

She shivered, although she wasn't cold. Boone wrapped her in his strong arms. "The story is still yours. They didn't reveal it and you still have time."

"How much time?"

Boone shrugged, his arms still around her. "I'm sure they'll contact your dad today."

"I should go home."

"No, you shouldn't. You're staying here. You're safe here. They want money, Kayla. But they also seem to want revenge. They're striking out, targeting you, because they know you're important to your dad."

"Right," she whispered, for the first time letting go of the newfound strength and faith. She felt weak down to her toes.

"You are important to him."

"I'm going to stir the eggs," Jase said. Kayla looked up, seeing concern in his brown eyes. She'd forgotten his presence.

"I'm sorry, Jase. You don't need this on a Saturday morning."

He winked. "I'm not worried about myself, Kayla."

"What do we do now?" she asked Boone.

"We talk to your dad. We see if his men have any clue who we're dealing with."

"And we eat a good breakfast. It's the most important meal of the day." This from Jase. Humor laced with a thread of concern, enough to ease the tension the tiniest bit.

They made it easy to smile, this family that had faced their own hardships but seemed to keep moving forward with smiles and love for each other.

A little over a week ago she'd been upset by this invasion of bodyguards into her life. A lot could change in a week. A person could change. Her heart could change.

And that opened a whole new world of possibilities.

Boone left the house after breakfast. His mom and sisters had Kayla busy, enlisting her to help prepare the twins for their pageant. He still didn't get the pageant, but Essie had explained about the scholarships and cash prizes.

Boone left them to it and headed for the barn and work he couldn't put off any longer. There was some serious bush hogging that needed to be done on a back field that had been overtaken by weeds during the hot, dry summer when it seemed weeds flourished and grass didn't. They also had some fence to fix and some calves to tag.

Jase and Lucas caught up with him when he was almost to the barn and thinking he might have a few minutes to himself. Lucas was talking about the Martin's Crossing Annual Ranch Rodeo that would be held in a week. He had signed them up for team penning and calf branding. He said it would be a good time to get those new calves branded. Jase and Boone just looked at each other and kept walking.

"What? Are we not going to participate this year?" Lucas kept at them, running backward in front of them to get their attention. "Are you going to let the Martins win again?"

"No, Lucas, we won't let the Martins win. No one lets them win. They just do it because they're good."

Lucas jerked off his hat with the bluster and energy of a teenager. "Oh, come on. We could beat them if we tried."

"We haven't been practicing. So it seems to me that not only do we not want to lose, we don't want to look like fools." Boone pushed his youngest brother to the side and Lucas moved in next to him as they walked.

Boone got it. He knew how hard it was for

their little brother. A lot had changed in the past few years. Boone had been gone, and then he'd returned home injured. Their dad had suffered a massive heart attack. That had left Lucas as the youngest boy, and the one not getting what the rest of them had: all of their dad's time and attention. It was the little things that mattered; Boone knew that. Which was why he was here, helping out.

"We can practice. We should start this evening," Lucas pushed.

"The Martins practice every day," Jase reminded.

"We used to. We can get back to it," Lucas pressed further. He wanted the old days back again. Boone wanted that, too. He'd like to just focus on the ranch, and not this crazy burning-the-candle-at-both-ends thing they were all doing. Jase in college and still living at the ranch, trying to keep everything running. Boone working the bodyguard business and the ranch. Lucas just trying to still be a kid.

"We'll practice tonight, Lucas," he promised. Even as he worried about what would possibly interfere, his phone rang. "I have to take this. Jase, check the tractor. Lucas, get ear tags and whatever else we need."

He lifted his phone to his ear. "Mr. Stanford. I guess you saw the news?" Boone answered as he walked away from his brothers.

"Yes, Wilder, I saw the news. Where's my daughter?"

"She's fine, sir, in case you were wondering."

There was a long pause. "Boone Wilder, I'm going to tell you this once. I do care about my daughter. And I don't owe you any explanations."

"No, sir, you don't." Boone leaned against the fence, watching cattle graze. They'd had to cut the herd to pay medical expenses when his dad had gotten sick. They were rebuilding it. And he wasn't going to lose this job. His family was counting on him.

He thought of Kayla. She was counting on him, too. He wasn't sure what he could do for her, but for whatever reason she'd been brought into his life and his home. People had been praying for her, he'd known that. Maybe this was the way God answered, the way she got help from people who cared.

"Mr. Wilder, I'm talking to you."

Boone cleared his throat. "Yes, I'm sorry, sir. You were saying."

"My daughter is important to me. I—" There was a heavy pause. "I made a mistake."

"I see" was all Boone could say.

"I'm going to withdraw from this campaign before they can tell everything. *If* they know everything. My investigators believe that someone who knows our story might be working for another candidate and this is how they're fighting. It's dirty, but I won't let them run my family into the ground."

"If this was just about politics, would your daughter be in danger?"

"They've definitely crossed the line. But I'm not going to pay them."

"I'm not sure your daughter wants you to quit the campaign, sir. She seems to remember a man who, at one time, wanted to help people."

Man, he'd just done it again. He couldn't seem to stay out of hot water with this guy.

"Wilder, you're fired."

"I understand."

"Bring my daughter back to Austin. We'll get another service to protect her."

Boone rubbed a hand over his face and sighed.

"Sir, I understand how you feel, and I have to apologize. But in all honesty, I think your daughter wants the best for you. And I think you want the same for her. She's safe here.

This is not the time to surround her with strangers and leave her on her own."

"Then, what do you suggest I do?" This time the voice had softened, making it a legitimate question, one of a concerned father.

Boone bit back about a half dozen less-than-decent replies and softened it down to one. "Maybe you should talk to her."

"I'm dealing with a lot here, Wilder." The other man let out a long sigh. "I'm going to be meeting with the police and my PI this afternoon. I have to stop this before it goes any further. But I'll be down there in a few days. Keep her close and keep her safe."

"I'm keeping her safe. That's why you pay me."

"Yes, and don't forget it. Next time I won't be so forgiving. Next time you're out of a job."

"I understand."

Boone slipped his phone in his pocket and turned to find Kayla standing a short distance away. "My dad?"

"Yeah."

She had changed into jeans, a T-shirt and what looked like a pair of Michaela's hand-me-down boots. Her dark hair was braided on the side and hung down over her shoulder. She looked like a country girl. And she looked relaxed.

"You don't have to handle him for me," she said. "My father, I mean."

"I know. But there's no sense allowing him to run you over."

"I rarely allow that, Boone."

He took a step toward her. "No, you don't. So what are you doing out here dressed like that?"

"I'm going to help you. Your mom is reading to your dad. Michaela ran into town with Molly to have a playdate. The twins have Janie cornered, doing something crazy to her hair."

"Janie will regret that. I let them do my hair once and ended up with highlights."

Her blue eyes sparkled with amusement and she reached out, brushing her hand down his cheek. "I like you. I didn't plan on that."

He hadn't planned on liking her, either. But then he hadn't known she was hiding this strength, and the flashes of humor. He hadn't planned on this crazy need to keep her safe, and to make her smile more often.

Warning bells went off in his head, telling him to get it together and reminding him she was just a job. She had a sad story but she was strong. She'd survive. She didn't need to be rescued. She needed to be kept safe.

He couldn't keep her safe if he got sidetracked, distracted.

"Say something," she said, looking a little worried, staring up at him.

What could he say? He was protecting her and someday soon she wouldn't be his client any longer. She'd go back to her life. Maybe she'd leave here a little a little happier and a little more whole.

"I like you, too," he finally said. And then he cleared his throat, uncomfortable with words that sounded as if he might have said them on the playground in grade school.

She snorted a laugh. "Said like a man who doesn't want to say too much."

"I'm your bodyguard, Kayla. And you've been on an emotional roller coaster for the past few weeks."

"More like for ten years. And you're right, I'm sorry. I was hoping we could be friends."

He could give her that. "I think we can be friends."

"Can I take a ride on your little green tractor?" She pointed to the tractor coming around the side of the barn, Jase behind the wheel.

"That I think I can arrange. I'm going to bush hog."

"Bush hog?" Her eyes narrowed. "I'm from the city, you have to explain."

"The mower attached to the back of the tractor. We're going to mow the field, cut down weeds and small shrubs."

"Oh, sounds like fun."

"It isn't," he assured her as they headed for the barn.

"About my dad. He knows?"

Boone adjusted his hat to shield his eyes from the sun. "Yeah, he knows. He said he'll pull out of the race before he will allow the rest to come out."

"He said that?" She sounded surprised.

"Yes. I also told him that I didn't think you'd want him to quit. That you want him to be the politician you believe he could be. The man who helps people."

"Ouch."

"Then he fired me."

Her eyes widened. "What? He didn't."

"He did. But I talked him out of it."

She slugged his shoulder. "You are a miserable creature."

"He's coming down to see you. Maybe in a few days."

She walked away from him, toward the tractor. Jase was climbing down, leaving the door open.

"Hey, Kayla. Did you come out to help with the cattle?" He tipped his hat back and gave her that big grin of his. Boone shook his head. One of these days his little brother's flirting was going to land him in hot water.

"Actually, I'm going to help bush hog." She glanced back at Boone. "Right?"

"If you say so." He wasn't going to argue. He stood back and watched as she managed to climb up into the cab of the tractor. "Don't touch anything."

"Like this?" She pushed a button. And then she shifted.

"Kayla, I mean it."

Suddenly the tractor was moving. Jase jumped back, leaving room for Boone to take a running hop, grab the handle and climb the steps. He slid into the seat beside her and brought the tractor to a stop.

"That. Wasn't. Funny."

"Sure it was." She pulled down on the brim of his hat. "The panic in your eyes was priceless. I've driven a tractor, Boone. My brothers are the Martins. Brody taught me last year.

And I know what a bush hog is. You're more gullible than you look."

"You're more trouble than *you* look," he quipped.

"You two going to kill each other?" Jase hollered up.

"Maybe," Boone said as Kayla leaned and said, "Of course not."

"I'll let you all decide. I'm going to saddle a horse, and Lucas and I will bring in the calves that need to be tagged. When we get that done, we'll be on the fence."

"Tell him work first, rodeo later," Boone called out to his brother's retreating back. Jase saluted and kept walking. Boone closed the tractor door, and the inside of the tractor turned into a quiet cocoon with country music playing softly on the radio.

"Not a lot of room in here," Kayla said. She shifted over, giving him a little more of the seat.

"No, they don't make tractors for two."

"They should if they're going to write songs about them."

He laughed and kept driving. "So Brody taught you to drive a tractor? Brave."

"He's my favorite."

"He's a good man."

A little while later she asked, "Is he angry? My dad, I mean."

"He's angry at the people who are doing this. Not you. He wants you safe. The problem with people like this, Kayla, is that they're desperate. And you never know what a desperate person is going to do next."

"I know."

"I'd like to stay with Sam. I know that isn't safe. But she's my sister. And she's a good shot."

"That isn't going to happen. We can visit tomorrow, maybe, after church."

"Okay."

They reached the field that needed clearing. He stopped the tractor and sat there for a minute.

"Seems a shame to cut that down, doesn't it?" he said.

The field had been overtaken by wildflowers. Butterflies hovered and a few tiny songbirds flitted from bush to bush. He cut the engine to the tractor and opened the door. Fresh autumn air swept through the cab.

"I think I'd rather take a walk in it than see it cut down," Kayla told him with a hopeful tone in her voice.

And he caved. "Let's go."

He climbed down and then held up a hand to help her. She didn't take the offer. She jumped down in a second, standing next to him. Her hand slipped into his, an easy gesture that shouldn't have taken him by surprise. But it did. In more ways than one.

"Maybe we could cut it after the first frost," he conceded as they walked.

"Good idea."

They walked as far as the creek. It was slow going. The wildflowers and weeds really had taken over. But it was wild and beautiful. This was what he'd missed about hill country during those long, dusty, hot months in Afghanistan.

The creek was running low, the way it usually did in the fall. He stood back and watched as Kayla slipped off her boots and rolled up the legs of her jeans.

"It's going to be cold," he warned.

"I don't care." She tiptoed into the water. "I've always wanted to do this."

"Your bucket list must be interesting."

She stood there in the ankle-deep water and his heart kind of lurched. She waded back out of the creek. She took the hand he offered, then sat down on the bank of the creek, pulling him down with her.

"My bucket list," she said. "Yes, it's interesting. I think at the top of the list was finding my family. And somehow finding myself again."

"Better than a trip to Paris."

"Been there, done that, Wilder. What about you?"

"Never been to Paris. Never really wanted to go. Getting this ranch back in the black. Making sure my dad is healthy again. I guess those are on my list."

"Those are goals, not a bucket list. You have to have one."

"Okay. I'd like to climb a mountain in Alaska. Maybe go deep-sea fishing. And I've always wanted to kiss a pretty girl while sitting on the bank of this creek." The words rushed out, making him feel like all kinds of a fool.

"So let's check that off our list today, Wilder." She leaned in, brushing her lips against his. "Because I think that might have been on my list, too. Kissed by a cowboy."

He could have backed away. He probably should have. But her fingers slid across the back of his neck and he took the invitation. She tasted like sweet tea and sunshine. And her hands on his neck gave him crazy thoughts.

He tugged that braid that hung down her shoulder and pulled her a little closer. His fingers wrapped around the braid, lifting it to inhale strawberry-scented shampoo.

"Kayla," he finally managed to whisper. "This is going to get us into all kinds of trouble."

"I know," she agreed.

"I'm the person trying to keep you safe, and I can't do that if I'm caught up in this, whatever *this* is."

"I'm sorry, Boone. I know this is wrong. I know this is the last thing you want or need." Hurt laced her tone. And hurting her was the last thing he wanted to do.

Which was why he had to back away and keep his focus. He'd never lost focus on a job this way before. Never been tempted the way she tempted him. He liked her. It all came down to that.

"This is the last thing *you* need, Kayla." He laced his fingers through hers. "We've got to keep you safe. And you have a life waiting for you."

She closed her eyes, her face caught in the sunshine. He leaned closer to her, but they didn't touch.

Her response came a few minutes later. She

opened her eyes and looked at him. "My life does seem as though it's been on hold for a while. But this is what I do. I rush into things. I rush because I want to feel."

He nodded silently.

"But you're right. I'm sorry for putting you in this position, that you have to be the person telling me to back off."

"Kayla, it isn't all you."

She sat up, her hand covering his. "Please don't do the 'it's not you, it's me' lecture."

With that he stood, holding out a hand to help her to her feet. "We should head back to the house and help the guys. And I'll try not to be embarrassed when I tell them I couldn't bear to cut down a field of wildflowers."

And he didn't know how to distance himself from the woman at his side.

Chapter Eight

Kayla watched from the sidelines of the somewhat weathered and worn arena where the Wilders were practicing for the ranch rodeo on Saturday evening. Lucas had insisted she come. They had one week until the event. They could do this, he'd insisted. Lucas was the family cheerleader. The one trying hard to get back what had been lost in the past few years.

She understood Lucas. She knew that drive to get back what she'd lost.

She hopped off the fence and went to sit on the low riser next to Maria and Michaela. Jesse Wilder was near the chutes coaching his children from a chair they'd brought out for him. She could hear him calling out to Lucas, his voice weak. Jase had a calf down and Janie was holding the branding iron, a circle W that had been used on the ranch since the first Wilder had settled in this area.

"Lucas, if you're going to brand calves, you have to be ready," Jesse Wilder called out, this time a little louder.

Lucas rode up on his horse, a pretty bay, black mane plaited in thick braids from her ears to the base of her neck. He must have spent hours doing all of that braiding. Kayla had to give him kudos for patience.

"Dad, I know what I'm doing." Lucas stayed in the saddle, swinging a lasso easily. He shot a look in the direction of his twin sisters. They were on their horses in the arena, but doing more laughing than working. "But you know we should just lock up those two and leave them at home."

"They're a part of this ranch, son."

"Then, Kayla should be out here with us. If she's staying on the Wilder Ranch, she should be one of the Wilder hands at the rodeo."

Gray haired but still charming, Mr. Wilder shot a look in her direction. "Well, Kayla?"

"No, thank you. There's no way I could help sort or brand calves. Or even stay in the saddle."

Jesse slapped his leg and laughed. "Oh, Kayla, I don't think you have enough faith in yourself. I bet you could outride this banty rooster son of mine."

"Hey," Lucas called out as he was riding away from his dad. "I resent that."

Mr. Wilder gave her a wink. And then he rubbed his chest, causing Maria to come up off the riser and head his direction.

"Jesse?"

He smiled up at his wife, but even Kayla could see that the gesture was a little less than genuine. "I'm good, Maria. Relax."

"I can't relax. You've been doing that too often lately."

"And I'm fine. Go sit with the girls. I'm going to give Lucas some tips on this branding business."

"You'll tell me if..." she started.

"If I need to be hauled off to the hospital, I'll let you know. But for now, sit down."

"You try my patience, Jesse." Maria leaned to kiss him. "I need you on this earth with me."

"I'm not going anywhere."

Maria gave him a long look. "Promise?"

"Promise."

She left him to go sit on the risers with her daughter and granddaughter, though reluctance was written all over her face. Kayla held on to that tough but bittersweet moment between husband and wife. A real ache settled in her heart, a need for something genuine and lasting.

She started back to the risers and the other women but was stopped by Boone.

"Hey, don't run off, Stanford." He was leading a pretty gray horse, the animal leaning in close to him. "I brought you something."

"I think you have the wrong woman." She backed up against the fence.

"Oh, no, I don't. We could use an extra hand for this rodeo." He pushed back the brim of his cowboy hat and a corner of his mouth tilted in a charming grin.

"Don't you try to charm me into this."

He leaned a little close. "Is it working?"

"Not at all," she said, but her heart disagreed. She was definitely charmed. His eyes were dark and a five-o'clock shadow covered his cheeks.

He wore his jeans low on his hips and his T-shirt hugged his shoulders. A silver chain with a tiny cross hung around his neck.

"Not even a little?" he teased in a quiet, husky voice.

"Not enough to get on that horse," she told him.

He laughed and took her by the hand. "Climb on, cowgirl. Let's get this show on the road."

"I can't ride."

"Yes, you can." A truck pulled up the drive, distracting them. She exhaled a relieved breath as Samantha's truck stopped next to the arena. Both Samantha and Brody climbed out of the truck. Brody, lean and dark haired. Samantha, blonde and confident. They were Kayla's siblings. Sometimes she had to stop for a minute and adjust all over again to the reality that she'd had this family all along and never knew about them until the past year. It was Brody's determination that had brought her into their lives.

Brody hurried forward and hugged her. "Hey, little sister. I've been thinking you might call me."

"I'm sorry, I should have."

Brody switched his focus to Boone. There was a sharp look between the two. "Boone."

"Brody." Boone just grinned. "As you can see, she's safe."

Brody gave her another look. "Yeah, I can see. So care to tell me what's going on?"

Samantha let out a long sigh, because she was used to these men. "Stop circling like old tomcats and remember that you're friends and on the same side. And, Kayla, feel fortunate you haven't put up with this your whole life."

Kayla pretended that was how she felt: fortunate. "What brings the two of you out here?"

Brody shot her a look. "You, of course. We're having lunch at Duke and Oregon's after church tomorrow. We'd like for you to join us."

"We'll be there," Boone answered for her.

"We?" Brody asked, one of his brows lifting.

"Where she goes, I go." Boone leaned against the saddle of the horse he'd led over. "Where I go, she goes. And I'm not passing up lunch at Duke's."

"Well, isn't that…" Brody started.

Boone stared him down. "That sounds like a man doing his job."

Brody chuckled.

Kayla took the reins of the horse Boone had brought for her. "If I'm going to learn to ride, we should get started."

From the arena, Lucas shouted at Jase. The

gray gelding next to Kayla startled. Boone reached for the reins and got the animal back under control.

"Those two brothers of mine," he muttered. He met her gaze and winked. "Brothers can be a real pain."

Brothers. Bodyguards. Yes, men could be a pain.

Boone's phone rang. He gave her an apologetic look and walked away. Samantha stepped forward, taking the reins from her and leading the horse a short distance from the arena.

"Come on, sis. If you're going to ride this animal, you have to get on his back. It works best that way." Sam shot her a cheeky look. "And keep your mind on the horse, not other things. Being distracted is a sure way to get tossed."

"I'm not distracted," Kayla assured her sister.

Sam's glance slid past Kayla, and she knew exactly who her sister thought might distract her. Boone.

No, Boone wasn't a distraction. He couldn't be. He was doing his job, keeping her safe. And as soon as the blackmailers were caught, she would go back to her life, back to Austin.

She belonged in the city. She couldn't wait to get back to her life. Not to the old life, but to the new one she planned on making for herself.

She definitely didn't need distractions.

Boone walked away from the arena, listening to the man on the other end of the phone tell him exactly what he'd do to Kayla Stanford, to her old man and even to Boone's family if someone didn't pay up. The stakes were being raised. The price was being raised. They had one week to come up with the money or the next article in the paper would give all of the details. And if that didn't convince Mr. Stanford, then they'd start playing rough.

It took everything Boone had to stay calm, to not yell at the man on the other end. The last thing he needed to do was get emotional, to show his hand. Calm, steady breaths. He listened as if they were talking about the weather.

"Interesting story, bud, but I'm kind of busy here." He grinned as he said it, as if the other man could see.

"Your old man is sick. And I'm just going to take a wild guess and say you're getting attached to your client."

He drew in a sharp breath at the mention of his dad. His gaze drifted toward the arena. His family was a short distance away, completely innocent, not a part of the Stanford family drama. But he said nothing. This wasn't going to get under his skin.

"Got something to say, Wilder?"

"No, not really. But I'll pass on your message to Mr. Stanford."

"You do that."

The phone went dead. He slipped it in his pocket and turned back to the arena. Brody appeared out of the shadows.

"Interesting phone call?" he asked.

Boone shrugged. "I guess you could say that."

"Threats?"

"A few. Nothing to worry about."

Brody walked next to him. "You look worried. If you're worried, then I guess I have a right to be."

"You can do what you want, Brody."

Brody stopped walking. "Boone, we're friends. We've been friends a long time. This is about my sister."

"Now they're threatening my family," Boone admitted. "And I'd say it's a matter of time before they threaten yours."

"Then, I guess someone needs to figure out who it is."

"Mr. Stanford has the police and a PI team on that. My job is to keep your sister safe."

"Can you keep her safe when Samantha has her out there in the arena, sorting calves?"

He glanced that way. Samantha was on his horse. She was riding next to her sister, the two of them laughing and carrying on like kids. He guessed they were more alike than he'd realized. Both were a little reckless, grabbing at life and running headlong into danger.

"She'll get thrown." He headed for the arena with Brody not hurrying behind him.

"She might, Boone, but she'll learn. We all learned by taking our falls and getting back on."

"Right, but I'm supposed to keep her safe. Not help her get her neck broke."

"Calm down." Brody laughed as he said it. "You're losing focus."

"I'm not." He started to defend himself, but then realized maybe he was. The call had rattled him. Seeing her on that horse, reckless but carefree, that rattled him, too.

And in the next instant the horse shied to the right and he watched as she toppled, landing hard on the packed dirt of the arena.

He was over the fence and heading for her as she sat up, shook her head and looked around as if she wasn't sure where she was. Samantha was off her horse.

"Crazy. Both of you are just crazy." He lowered himself next to her.

"Get a grip, Boone." Samantha reached out a hand and pulled her sister to her feet. "You okay?"

"Sore, but I don't think anything is broken." Kayla rubbed her shoulder. "I didn't see that coming."

Boone stood, looking at the two of them. He saw resemblances. He saw differences. He felt something crazy deep inside that shouldn't be there.

"Of course you didn't see it coming. You were distracted." As he said the words, they hit him hard, reality shaking him to the core.

"She's fine. You're fine, right?" Sam asked.

"I'm fine."

Jase appeared at his side. "Anything broken?"

Kayla shook her head. "I hit my shoulder, but I think it's okay."

Jase touched her arm, touched her shoulder. Boone fought emotions that he wasn't about to put a name to. Lucas rode up, whistling, long and appreciative.

"That was quite a buck-off, Kayla."

She grinned up at him. "Thanks, Lucas."

"I think we should call it a night," Boone suggested. Not only because of her fall but because he had a strange feeling that they were being watched. The hairs on the back of his neck stood up and he couldn't quite dislodge the fact that someone knew too much about all of them.

"Let's go inside for tea," Jase offered, shooting Boone a questioning look. "Me, Lucas and the twins can get these horses cooled off and put up for the night. You all go on in."

"Thanks, Jase." Boone reached for Kayla but she was already moving ahead of him, her arm through Samantha's. Brody stepped in next to him.

"I remember the first time she showed up at Jake's. Crazy in that red convertible of hers. She's changed a lot in the past year. Having family has done that for her." Brody glanced around as they walked. "Do you think you're being watched?"

"Why do you ask?"

"Because I know you well enough to know

that look in your eyes. You're cautious, Boone, but you're watching everything all at once."

"I'm doing my best." Ahead of them, his mom was helping his dad up the stairs. Michaela and Molly were waiting for them up ahead. "I think Kayla and I need to sit down and make a list of people who might know…"

"Know what?" Brody asked, his trademark smile dissolving. "What aren't you telling me?"

"Nothing. Someone knows how to get under her father's skin. We need to figure out who that person is."

"And you're not going to tell me anything else?"

Boone watched the front door close behind Kayla and Samantha, leaving him and Brody standing in the front yard alone.

"No, I'm not going to tell you anything else."

"The story in the paper implied there's more. Now you're implying it, too. If there's something that needs to be dealt with, maybe you should tell Kayla's family."

"Brody, that isn't my place and you know it." He headed up the steps and Brody followed. "I'm keeping her safe."

"Yeah, I know you are."

They entered the kitchen to find Kayla sitting on a stool, an ice pack on her shoulder. Boone removed the ice and pushed up the short sleeve of her T-shirt to take a look. He touched the bruise that had developed and she flinched.

"Ouch, Wilder."

"Sorry, Stanford. That's going to hurt tomorrow."

She moved, dislodging his hand. "Why do people always say, 'It's going to hurt tomorrow'? You know something? It hurts right now."

"I guess we just want you to know it's going to be worse before it gets better," he shot back.

She rolled her eyes at him, those big blue eyes. "Thanks, Wilder, your encouragement means everything."

Her voice sounded too tight, too emotional. He wanted to laugh it off, make it all a joke.

"That's what I'm here for," he said.

"I'm glad we all know why we're here," Brody Martin said as he pinned Boone with a look. "Wilder, the reason you're here is to keep my sister safe."

Boone leaned against the counter, crossed his arms over his chest and glared at Brody. Obviously Brody had forgotten that Boone was a few years older, and a few inches taller. It hadn't been too many years ago that the two of them had gone at each other. With Brody on the losing end of the fight. All in good fun, of course.

He winked at Kayla, then turned his attention back to her brother.

"I think you can go home, Brody. We're good."

"You have someone helping?" Brody asked.

"Daron. I'm assuming he's at my place and if not, he'll be back soon. And we'll see you all at church tomorrow."

Brody shifted his attention from Boone to Kayla. "You're sure you're okay?"

"I'm good, Brody. I'm sure that it won't be the last time I get thrown."

Brody leaned against the counter, looking down at her. "I don't mean getting tossed, Kayla. I want to know that you're okay and if there's anything we can do. You have family now."

"I'll let you know. But you should go. Grace will be wondering where you are," Kayla stated with simple ease. And it was enough to get Brody's attention. It even put some kind of strange smile on his face that Boone never would have pictured there. It was the look of a man completely in love with his wife and baby.

Boone pushed down a strange spike of jealousy that he hadn't expected. He didn't need complications. He glanced around the big country house at the family that depended on him. His mom was in the kitchen, making a batch of brownies with Molly's help. Michaela was holding her daughter as Molly stirred. The twins were in the living room arguing, as usual. It was his family that kept him grounded, kept him here doing what needed to be done.

His gaze connected with Kayla's. Their smiles touched in a way that nearly undid him. It felt as if she'd reached out and brushed his heart with that smile.

He wasn't a poetic sort of guy, not normally. But it moved him, that smile of hers. Boone walked closer to her. She glanced up at him, her eyes widening.

The gesture didn't go unnoticed. Of course it didn't. Not with his mom and sister present. Not with Samantha and Brody Martin standing not five feet away. And yet, even with everyone around them, he couldn't help but brush his fingers across hers, a brief gesture that seemed to suck the air right out of him.

From across the room, Brody cleared his throat. "Well, if you've got things handled here, I'm heading home."

"Things are handled," Boone assured his friend.

"Yeah, it looks as if they are." Brody headed for the front door, Samantha trailing next to him with a last look back and a smile for her sister.

Boone walked them out, because he'd been raised to be polite. And because Brody and Sam had been friends of his for years. Things would get back to normal. Kayla would go back to her life in Austin with occasional visits to the Martin ranch, and her family. Boone would see her from time to time. Or not.

He was almost thirty, and for the first time in a long time, that "or not" part bothered him. He didn't know how Kayla had managed to twist him up like a ball of twine in just a couple of weeks, but she had.

There were a whole lot of reasons the two of them were a bad idea. She was city. He was as country as they came. He was her bodyguard. She was his client. This was just about the worst time for him to feel as though he wanted to take this girl to dinner, maybe more than once.

Chapter Nine

Sunday morning Boone left the rest of his family fighting over the two bathrooms they shared and headed for his RV. It was the best kind of fall morning, a little bit cool and the smell of drying grass in the air. On a morning like this one, he could almost forget the troubles knocking at their door. He could let himself forget about unpaid medical bills, his dad's health problems and the complication that was Kayla Stanford.

He took a deep breath as he walked the worn path, Sally coming to greet him with a low and familiar woof. He ran a hand over her head. In response she gave him a soft look of loyalty. "This is why you're the woman for me, Sally."

A familiar Ford King Ranch was parked

in front of his RV. "But you could be a better guard dog and run him off," he told her. She trotted off, completely oblivious.

As he walked up the steps of his trailer, he glanced at his watch. He had thirty minutes to get ready, and Daron had better not be hogging his bathroom. His mom had given him the warning look before he'd headed out. They weren't going to be late today, she'd informed them all at breakfast. Because the Wilders did tend to be late. Often. There were a lot of them and that meant fighting over bathrooms. Even with the schedule their mom had posted on the fridge, they were always trying to sneak in during someone else's allotted time. They were a rowdy bunch, he guessed. And probably something of a novelty to someone like Kayla Stanford.

The smell of burned eggs greeted him as he walked through the door of the trailer. Great, Daron was cooking again. That never ended well. The kitchen was a mess. There were dirty dishes, a pan in the sink with scorched scrambled eggs, and something that looked like it might have been sausage was in the dog's bowl. The dog whined and then nudged at what appeared to be a burned offering.

Loud, off-key singing overwhelmed the

music on the radio. The dog looked up at Boone, one ear lifted.

"He has to go, right, Sally?" Boone asked the dog.

The singing stopped. A few minutes later Daron walked down the hall, his hair still damp. "Oh, hey. I didn't know you were back. I made breakfast."

"Yeah, I know. The government called. They asked that you stop making weapons of mass destruction."

"Very funny."

"Seriously, don't cook again. Ever. My mom made a five-course breakfast."

Daron tossed his towel over the back of a chair and reached for his boots. "I'm not going to mooch off your parents."

Boone gave him a look.

Daron laughed it off. "I don't mind mooching off you. You're my friend."

"That's debatable. I've got to jump in the shower and get ready for church. Why don't you button that shirt and pretend you're civilized. You can ride with me to church and join us for lunch later."

"I think God and I have other things to work out," Daron grumbled as he headed for the door. "I have to make a run to Austin."

"Maybe you ought to stop that running. Slow down a little."

Daron stopped at the door. "You fix yourself, Boone Wilder. I'll fix me."

"Yeah, okay." Boone sat down to remove his prosthesis. "So how is she?"

"She?" Daron stood with the door open. "I don't know who you mean."

"Can we stop dancing around this subject? Emma. How is she?"

Daron glanced out the door, his smile long gone. "Poor. Alone. And doing her best to raise Jamie."

"He should have married her."

"He's dead, so no reason to throw stones now."

Boone conceded that point. "Yeah, I know. She still chasing you off the place with that rusted-out shotgun?"

Daron grinned. "Yep. She says I don't owe her anything. I think I do."

"We all feel as if we owe someone, don't we?" Boone stood, holding the edge of the table to balance.

"I guess we do. Who do you owe?"

Boone turned away from his friend. "You'd better go."

"Yeah, all right. Be careful. I'll be around tomorrow to give you a break."

"That would be good. I've got to get some work done around here."

Daron waved a hand and walked out the door. Boone watched from the kitchen window as his friend climbed in his truck and headed off down the drive, throwing a little dust and gravel in his wake. After a few minutes he hopped down the hallway, trying not to get caught up in Daron's pain, in his past.

They all had stuff to deal with.

When Boone pulled up to his folks' house shortly before ten, the family was spilling out the door and heading for the big van that hauled them all. He parked behind the van and got out, wincing a little at the jab of pain he hadn't been expecting. His sister Michaela shot him a look. With a grin and a wink he pushed aside her concern and headed for Kayla. She was waiting her turn to climb into the van.

"You'll be riding with me," he informed her.

She gave him a dark look, her blue eyes arctic. He just smiled, because he knew that would rile her more than anything he had to say. She was a tall woman, he realized, not for the first time. Tall and too thin. Her dark hair was pulled back and wispy curls framed her face. But he was her bodyguard, not her date.

"In the car, sunshine." He motioned her toward his truck.

"I'll ride in the van with everyone else," she countered.

"And make me ride to town all alone? That wouldn't be charitable of you."

She let out a sigh, the kind that was meant to tell him just how put out she was. But when he put a hand on her arm to guide her to his truck, she went with him. A quick glance back, he caught his mom's gaze on them, her eyes narrowed. Yeah, she would worry. He wished he could find a way so that she could do less of that. He would like to give her a year of no worries, for anyone or anything. It wasn't realistic, he knew that, but it seemed like worry should be equally distributed. One woman shouldn't get more than her share.

He opened the truck door for Kayla but she didn't get in. Instead, she gave him a more pleading look, the kind that tugged at a guy's heart. "Please, just let me stay here. I'm not going to leave."

"I'm not worried about you leaving, Kayla.

I'm worried because someone is stalking you. I don't want you hurt."

Her eyes widened, telling him more with that look than she'd told him with words. She didn't expect him to care. When was the last time she expected anyone to care? She bit down on her bottom lip, then turned to get in the truck. "Boone, don't act as if this is more than a job."

What was he supposed to say to that?

"Kayla, this *is* more than a job. And I'm not going to let anyone hurt you."

"Too late," she whispered, then climbed into the truck and reached to close the door.

On the way to church Boone tried not to think about those two words she'd spoken. *Too late.* That had opened up something. He could see it in her expression, in the tension of her shoulders.

The last thing he wanted was to be the person who hurt her.

They pulled up at Martin's Crossing Community Church. The parking lot was overflowing and someone was ringing the bell. He parked and got out, but he was starting to feel as if this was a bad idea.

When he opened her door she looked up, one tear trickling down her cheek before she swiped it away and put on a big smile.

He'd spent a few years getting his life together and not getting involved with anyone. That tear sliding down her pale face just about undid all of his resolve. Yup. He was involved, no two ways about it.

"Don't worry, I'm not falling apart." With those words she got out of his truck and took his hand.

Boone led her through the front door of the building. As they walked past a pew he noticed a box of tissue. He grabbed the box and handed it to her.

"The whole box?" She laughed, but it was shaky. "I'm not going to lose it. It's nothing, so don't get all he-man on me."

"I just thought you might want to blow your nose. You're a mess."

She laughed again, but the laughter didn't stop the silent fall of tears sliding down her cheeks.

"Stop laughing like that, Stanford. You'll have people convinced you like me."

She pulled a tissue from the box and wiped her eyes. "I doubt it."

"Okay, they'll think I made you cry." He led her to an empty pew and motioned her in ahead of him. "People see what they want to see."

She gave him a long, careful look. "What do you think they see, Boone? When they look at you, what do they see?"

Good for her, turning the tables on him. "They see a guy who takes his family and his career very seriously. A guy who can keep you safe."

"I believe that, too."

The way she said it surprised him. And worried him. He didn't want to let her down.

The pew filled up. Which meant she had to move closer to Boone's side. Closer to the protection of his body, to the scent of his cologne. Closer to a realization about herself. For years she'd been running from her pain and herself. It had taken this situation, this man, to force her to confront the past. He'd helped her open up because he knew how to be quiet and listen.

There was no way to run, not this time.

After her mom's death she had run from her siblings, from the very people who could have helped and would have been there for her. She was her own worst enemy. She knew that about herself. There might be a stranger threatening to expose secrets, seeking money, but the things she could have and had done to herself were far worse.

That was then. This was now.

When she'd returned home from that trip to Mexico she'd entered rehab. Twelve steps to a new life. One step closer to God. It hadn't been easy, laying down everything before God: all the dirty little secrets, her shame, her anger, her pain.

But God already knew. Or so she'd been told. He knew her heartache. Knew her past and her future. Her sponsor had told her that God could make something beautiful from the ashes of her life.

That same sponsor had given the analogy that she should see herself as a broken vase. God was the glue to put her back together. Kayla thought it was a sweet story, but in truth there were pieces missing, so how could she ever be truly whole?

The service ended with a prayer. Kayla bowed her head and closed her eyes, needing that moment to pull herself together. She knew how to smile and pretend none of it mattered. She knew how to act as if it hadn't touched her at all. But she needed a minute to pull on her all-smiles mask.

But the service had touched her. It had felt

like a continuation of her talk with Maria Wilder, when Maria had prayed with her and told her to give herself and God a chance. Maria had also told her to forgive her dad. Forgive him, not just for him, but for herself. She had shaken off that suggestion. She was too angry to forgive. He didn't need or want her forgiveness because he didn't believe he'd done anything wrong.

A hand tightened on hers. As she stood, Boone's hand went to her back. It felt strangely protective. And she noticed he was on alert. His eyes darted to the back of the church and quickly took in the crowd.

"Do you think my stalker is going to show up here? In the middle of Nowhere, Texas?" she asked as he guided her through the church.

"I'm not taking any chances." He pointed. "There's your sister."

"Oh, that's right, lunch. We don't have to go."

"No, we don't. But we're going. I'm not letting you out of lunch with your family."

"I don't want to keep you from your family."

"You're not keeping me from anything, Stanford. There're so many of us Wilders, Mom won't notice one or two of us missing."

Samantha was upon them, her smile bright,

her hug long and suffocating. "I was afraid you'd skip out on us."

"I wouldn't dream of it."

"Oh, yes, you would." Samantha gave her another quick hug and then directed her attention to Boone. "You look, glum. No offense."

"Sam, if I took offense every time you ran me down, I'd be hiding in a corner somewhere trying to find my self-esteem."

"The two of you are coming over for lunch, correct?" Sam asked.

Boone didn't respond. He gave her a look, letting her know it was her decision to make.

"Yes, we're coming over." Kayla let her gaze slide to Boone. But he wasn't paying attention, not to her. He was watching the dwindling crowds, attentive and focused.

"Earth to Boone," Kayla teased.

He flicked her a look, accompanied by a frown.

"He's playing bodyguard," Kayla said in a stage whisper.

Boone gave her one of his well-meaning looks. She found them entertaining. This one told her he had a job to do. And she wasn't helping.

"I do take my job seriously, Stanford. And in case you forgot, this isn't a game."

"I know, I'm sorry."

Samantha cleared her throat. "Okay, then, we'll see the two of you at Duke's?"

"Yes, at Duke's."

Kayla would have said more to her sister, but Boone took hold of her arm and guided her toward the side exit, not the main doors.

"What are we doing?" she asked.

"Changing things up." He kept walking, his hand firm on her elbow.

"Boone, stop. You're starting to scare me."

He didn't slow down. "You should be scared."

"Why? I have you, right? You're the best. And whoever is doing this is just out for money. They aren't after anything else."

He kept walking, not answering her questions. When they got to the back door of the church, he stepped out first, looking both ways. He pulled her close to his side. "Stay close with me, Kayla."

"I'm with you."

They headed for the truck, not stopping to talk to people who called out. She tried to wave, to smile an apology. He didn't give her time. When they got to his old truck, he pulled the door open and practically lifted her inside.

"What is wrong with you?" she asked as he got behind the wheel.

"I got a text."

"You could have said something."

He started the truck and backed out of the parking space. "I didn't really want to take time to explain to you that we need to leave."

"What was the text?"

"The person who texted me knew what you were wearing and wanted to prove, they said, that they could get close to you."

She shivered, even though she tried to tell herself she wasn't afraid. For weeks she'd been telling herself this was all nothing more than an overzealous prankster. But it wasn't. Someone out there wanted to hurt her. They wanted to hurt her dad.

"It has to do with money and politics. So why doesn't my dad just pay them off?"

"Because they won't stop, Kayla. They'll take the money, and next time they'll raise the stakes. They'll always want more. They'll always want another payday. The only way to stop them is to figure out who they are."

"Someone my dad knows. Someone who knows me. Someone who wants him out of the race. But how do they know? It has to be someone close to our family. Or someone who worked for my dad."

He glanced her way just enough to give her a reassuring look. "We'll figure it out."

The drive to the Martin ranch was too quick. Kayla's brain was still scrolling through people she knew, or people her dad had known. Suspicions landed on those closest to her. Even her little brother Michael became a suspect. She couldn't imagine him doing this. He might want to hurt her, but never their father.

"You okay?" Boone questioned as they got out of the truck at Duke's house.

"I'm good, just thinking. Or trying not to think."

His hand was on her back. "Let it go for the day. You're safe. Your dad is safe."

"Is he?" And did she care? She'd spent so many years telling herself she didn't. But what if something happened to him?

"He's safe. He has a great team of security people surrounding him."

"Right, of course he does."

They were met at the front door by Oregon, Duke's wife. Her daughter, Lily, popped up behind her. Kayla greeted them with smiles and hugs. They were her family. Lily was her niece. There were other nieces and nephews. It was amazing that these people were her family. And she loved them.

They were pieces of the broken life that was being made whole.

"Come on in." Oregon led them through the sprawling, two-story farmhouse that she and Duke had remodeled. "Duke's on the grill out back. The others are sitting on the patio. It's such a perfect fall day."

"Would you like to see our new kittens?" Lily took hold of Kayla's hand. "They need homes."

"I'm not sure if getting a cat is a good idea right now," Kayla said, but her objections were ignored. Lily led her through the house, away from Oregon and Boone. "They're in the laundry room. I convinced Dad they have to be inside."

"But they don't?" Kayla guessed.

Lily grinned. "Not at all. But they're cute and the little kids love them."

She was petting a pretty gray ball of fluff when Samantha found them.

"Don't let her trick you into taking one of those kittens home," Sam warned.

"I'm not a cat person," Kayla felt confident in saying.

"Of course you're not." Sam picked up a dark gray tabby and held it close. "This one is mine. Not that I need another cat. Remington said we aren't even married and we already have a zoo."

"He loves you so much, he'd let you bring home a zoo," Kayla countered. "Another month until the wedding."

"I know. I thought I had months to prepare and then I woke up and realized I have days."

"Weddings and babies," Lily groaned. "This whole family is obsessed with weddings and babies. You know, there are teenagers. We live. We breathe. We were here first."

Sam ruffled their niece's dark hair. "Yes, Lily, you came first. We need to go. Lunch is ready."

Lunch was typical of the Martins, Kayla thought. There was a lot of laughter, a lot of talking. They ate outside where there were a couple of patio tables and plenty of chairs. Jake's wife, Breezy, sat down in the seat next to Kayla, a plate balanced on her lap and a glass of iced tea in her hand.

Kayla liked Breezy. She was earthy, quiet and genuine. And anyone could see that she was exactly what Jake Martin had needed. He was the serious older brother.

"You know, when this is over, you could always stay here," Breezy said, just as Sam arrived with her plate. Boone was a short distance away talking to Remington and Brody about the upcoming ranch rodeo and Lucas.

When Lucas was mentioned, Lily's eyes lit up. Oregon noticed it, too. She didn't look as amused. Lily was young. Too young for Lucas. That didn't mean she couldn't have a crush on the younger Wilder.

"Kayla?" Breezy cleared her throat.

"Sorry, just thinking. And I'm sure I'll just go home to Austin and go back to my life when this is all over." Back to what life? She looked up, saw the same question lurking in the eyes of her sister and sister-in-law. The life that was going nowhere? The life that counted for nothing?

"That sounds promising," Sam said with her customary honesty and a touch of sarcasm.

"Thanks," Kayla shot back. "Actually, I do have this pesky little degree in early childhood education. I could finish up, get certified and be a teacher. If there's a school that would have me."

From a short distance away Boone heard and arched one dark brow. She glared and went back to the conversation with her sisters. Oregon had joined them. She pulled up a chair and sat down.

"Martin's Crossing has a nice school," Oregon offered.

"I don't think Martin's Crossing is ready for me," Kayla answered. "And I'm not sure if I could live in the country. I've always lived in the city. It's just who I am."

This time she avoided looking at Boone, because she didn't want to see his reaction to the conversation. It shouldn't matter what he thought.

But deep down, she knew that it did.

Chapter Ten

Kayla was up at sunrise Monday morning. Early to bed, early to rise seemed to make Kayla Stanford healthy, happy and wise. Because she was happy. It was the strangest thing, to be here in the home of strangers, dependent on their kindness and charity, and yet she was happy.

She slipped out of her room just as Janie was coming out of her bedroom down the hall. Janie, always quiet and self-conscious. Kayla smiled at the younger woman.

"I'm getting used to this 'crack of dawn' business," Kayla said as the two of them walked downstairs together.

"I would love to sleep late," Janie responded. "I try, but I can't. I'm just used to being up early."

Maria Wilder was already up. She had a pot of coffee started and she was sitting at the kitchen table. Janie gave her a look, because Maria sitting down was unusual.

"Mom, you okay?"

Maria nodded. "I'm good. Maybe a little under the weather. I think I have that virus Molly had last week."

Janie put a hand to her mother's brow. "You're warm. Go back to bed."

"I have too much to do," Maria argued.

"And you have a house full of daughters who can do those things. The guys are working cattle today. The twins are upstairs practicing their pageant walk." She laughed at that and so did Maria. "Go back to bed. Let us be in charge for once."

"I can help," Kayla offered. Both Janie and Maria looked up. Kayla smiled, enjoying their looks of astonishment.

"Of course she can," Janie jumped right in. "We'll thaw something out for dinner, get the laundry going. Trust us."

Kayla grinned at Maria. "Yes, trust me."

Maria reached for her hand. "I do trust you, Kayla. Completely. So I'm going back to bed and I'm leaving the two of you in charge. Michaela has work today, so Molly will be here with you."

That seemed to take Janie by as much surprise as it took Kayla. "Molly?"

"Yes, your niece. Have fun."

Maria left the two of them standing in the kitchen looking at each other. Kayla laughed first.

"We're babysitting."

Janie shuddered. "Molly is a terror."

"I heard that." Michaela entered the room with her daughter. Molly waggled along next to her on pudgy legs, her blond hair in pigtails. She looked like a little darling. But then she smiled and all orneriness broke loose.

"Mom's gone back to bed. She has Molly's virus. We told her we'd hold down the fort today." Janie held a hand out to her niece. "So you're staying with us, Mols."

Molly didn't look thrilled.

"Mom is sick enough to go back to bed?" Michaela picked up her daughter. "That's unheard of."

"She deserves a break," Janie countered. "Molly, do you want oatmeal for breakfast?"

"Cookies." Molly grinned as she said it.

"No cookies." Michaela handed her daughter over to her sister. "Do not let her have cookies for breakfast. I have to run. Keep an eye on her. Do not let her out of your sight."

"Because I'm twenty and obviously don't know that." Janie snuggled her niece. "Go."

Michaela left, giving them each a warning look before heading out the door. Janie immediately passed the toddler to Kayla.

"Cookies," Molly said with a toddler lisp.

"I don't think we should have cookies for breakfast." Kayla held the little girl close.

The doorbell rang. Janie peeked out and then opened it. "Hey, Daron. Long time no see."

Tall, with sun-streaked hair and an air of confidence that he'd probably possessed since birth, Daron McKay was not on the list of Kayla's favorite people. Older than her by five years, they'd seen each other at social functions their fathers had insisted they attend but they'd never been friends. "Surprise," he said. "Kayla, don't look so happy to see me. I'm giving Boone a break. He's working cattle with the boys. I'm on Kayla duty."

"You're just in time for breakfast," Janie offered. She headed for the kitchen and Daron motioned for Kayla to go first. "I'm going to make pancakes."

"I love pancakes," Daron called back to

her. He stepped close to Kayla. "I talked to your father this morning. I want you to look at some photographs from old news stories. This person seems to have been around when you were in Mexico, and also Florida. Maybe you'll recognize someone."

"Sure." Kayla shifted Molly to her left hip. The little girl patted her cheek and kissed her.

Daron grinned. "I wouldn't have guessed you for a kid person, Kayla."

"Me, neither. She just doesn't know any better."

"Give yourself a break, will you?" he spoke sharply. "You've gotten used to being down on yourself."

"Yeah, I guess I have." She nuzzled the little girl in her arms. "Maybe I am a kid person."

He winked and took Molly from her. "Maybe you're a person who fixes me breakfast."

"Don't push it."

It was noon when Lucas and Boone came in for lunch. Jase had class on Mondays, so it was the two of them trying to separate calves that were ready to be weaned. Then they were heading back out to work on some fence that was starting to lean. Boone pulled off leather gloves and tossed them on the table. He glanced from Daron to Kayla.

"Have you showed her the photographs?"

"Not yet. She's been babysitting." Daron got up from the table. "I'll get my computer."

"Babysitting?" Boone asked as he pulled lunch meat out of the fridge. He eyed the slow cooker. "Where's Mom?"

"She's sick," Kayla explained. She pulled plates out of the cabinet. One for him. One for Lucas. "Janie and I are taking care of things."

"Where's Janie?" he asked.

"Trying to get Molly to take a nap."

Lucas laughed as he put a sandwich together. "That's not going to happen. That little girl has more energy than all of us combined."

"Mom's sick?" Boone asked again, his brows drawing together. "That never happens."

"Molly had a virus. They think your mom has the same."

"And Dad?" Boone asked as he sat down at the table with his plate. Kayla sat next to him.

"We took him lunch a little while ago. He's up and around but sitting with her. I think they're enjoying a quiet day, just the two of them."

"Yeah, I guess that isn't something they get too much of. Time alone."

Daron returned with his laptop. He set it on the table in front of Kayla. She glanced up, wishing this whole mess away. Before she could say anything, Janie appeared with Molly. The little girl was clinging to her neck and wiping tears off her cheek with a pudgy hand.

"She won't take a nap."

Lucas stepped into the room. "You just figured that out? She is not a napper."

Molly lifted her blond head off Janie's shoulder and pinned Kayla with her big eyes. "Kayka."

Janie handed the little girl over. "You're the new favorite."

"But I'm—" she held the little girl close "—not a kid person. Really."

Boone picked up his plate and carried it to the sink. "I guess you are now, *Kayka*."

Daron booted up his computer. "Here, babysitter, have a seat."

She sat next to him, Molly against her shoulder. Boone pulled out the chair on the other side of her. Lucas and Janie made excuses about other things to do. Janie was going to fold laundry. Lucas thought he'd work with his horse while he waited for Boone.

"I pasted photos so I have them all in one

file." Daron opened the folder and slid the computer in front of Kayla.

As she clicked through the photos, the little girl in her arms grew heavier. She shifted the sleeping child, Molly's head resting against her shoulder.

"So much for not wanting to take a nap," Boone said. "Do you want me to take her? I can put her on the sofa."

"No, I have her." She wouldn't have thought it could happen, but Molly had snatched up a piece of her heart. Holding her felt good. She inhaled the sweet scent of baby shampoo and brushed her cheek against Molly's soft hair.

"That's how it happens, Stanford. They lure you in when you're least expecting it." Boone leaned in to look at the pictures, but his shoulder brushed hers. She could have told him that Molly wasn't the only one luring her in. He was doing his share, and so was his family.

She would eventually have to leave this sweet place, and she knew that she'd miss it. Miss this family. Miss Boone.

"Whoa," Daron said as she clicked through pictures.

"What?"

"Back that up. Tell me who that is, around the bonfire."

She looked at the picture, a group of people around a fire. Big deal. Daron pointed. "That one."

Her heart stammered a little as she studied the picture. The face familiar, but not. She met Boone's gaze and he shrugged. Daron tapped the screen, making the image larger.

"I've met him but I can't remember his name. But I do know he's the nephew of Clarence Jacobs," Daron said quietly, letting it sink in.

"Clarence Jacobs is running against my dad. But I don't know him. So he wouldn't know anything about me." She closed her eyes, trying to force calm, trying to remember.

Boone took Molly from her arms and this time she let him. He soothed the little girl with softly spoken words as he carried her from the room.

"What would he gain from this?"

Daron leaned back, still looking at the photograph. "Money. But I can't imagine he needs any. Retribution?"

"For what?"

"Do you remember meeting him, Kayla?"

She closed her eyes, trying to bring back memories of that night. "I don't know. I must have, but I don't remember ever having a conversation with him. And it isn't as if I tell complete strangers what happened to me."

Or did she?

"It's great that she recognizes him and he's connected to politics," Boone said as he walked back into the room. "But you need more than that to arrest a guy for assault and extortion."

"Right." Daron attached a portable printer to his computer. "I'll take this to town and we'll see if we can't tie Mr. Wonderful to the phone calls, to the attacker, or even put his location near here."

"I don't even know his name," Kayla said. "I wish I could remember. A person should remember something this important."

Boone pulled her close, his arms strong. She leaned her head against his shoulder. She'd like to think she was a different person now. If she could believe anything about herself, she would believe that she was someone a man like Boone Wilder would take home to meet his family. Instead, she was the person hiding inside their home, hiding her real self, and trying to be someone they could accept.

"Stop," he whispered close to her temple, his breath soft against her skin.

"Stop what?"

Daron packed up his computer and the portable printer. He looked from Kayla to Boone, his eyes narrowing. "I'm heading to Austin. You've got this?"

Boone nodded, his chin brushing the top of her ear. "We're good."

He left with one last look for Boone. And Kayla knew that look. He was warning Boone to not get emotionally involved. Because she wasn't good for someone like Boone.

"Stop," Boone repeated, tightening his arms around the woman he held.

She turned in his embrace and looked up, her blue eyes tangling with his. A man could get lost in those eyes of hers.

"Stop blaming yourself," he continued. "Stop this trip into the past. It'll get you nowhere."

"But I can't undo who I was or the choices I made."

"No, you can't. But you can move forward. I think you have a clear idea of who you want to be. I think you've always known that person, but you tried to destroy her. Maybe you thought you couldn't be her."

"That woman would have been crushed by..." She shook her head and stepped away from him. "It was easier to pretend it didn't hurt."

"But it did hurt. You can't pretend the pain away, Kayla. You have to confront it. And you have to give yourself a chance to live."

"I know." She brushed a hand over her face. "But I'm tired, Boone. I'm so tired. I thought I'd escaped that life, but it came after me."

"We'll conquer it again. And again, if we have to. We'll keep conquering until you're free of it."

"What if I'm never free?"

He brushed a hand down her arm and she sighed at his touch. That encouraged him. He pulled her close again. "You are free. 'Whom the Son sets free is free indeed.' Kayla, you're free from the past. You've been redeemed. That doesn't mean you won't have battles. We all have battles."

She placed a hand on his cheek. "You have battles?"

"Yeah, I have battles."

He battled guilt. He battled his brain, making him think and rethink that day over and over again. People had been hurt and a man had died because Boone had trusted a kid. What kind of world did we live in that you couldn't trust a child?

Yes, he had battles. But the person he'd had to learn to forgive the most was himself.

He knew Daron fought the same battles. His guilt kept him tied to that day, to memories of a woman and to the life of another woman.

"I'm sorry, I shouldn't have forced you back there, Boone."

He blinked away the images of that day in Afghanistan. "I'm good."

Her smile was timid and sweet, shaking something loose inside him. For a dangerous minute he forgot that he was standing in his mother's kitchen, where any number of people could interrupt. It didn't seem to matter when she stood so close he could smell strawberry shampoo.

His hand went around her waist. His lips touched hers. She tasted like lemonade and sugar cookies. Her hand touched his neck, pulling him a little bit closer.

The kiss lingered, then she pulled away but stayed in his arms. She whispered, "We shouldn't do this."

"You're probably right." He let out a shaky breath. He knew it was wrong.

Focus, Boone. He gave himself a mental shake.

He told himself he wasn't going to fall for a client. He wasn't going to fall for a woman who had no interest in country life. The woman in his arms came from a life of wealth, of ease. She'd been raised in mansions, given every opportunity. His life was all about making do and keeping the ranch going. Opposites might attract, but that didn't mean they fit into each other's worlds.

Footsteps, heavy and too obvious, grew closer. He stepped away from her. A second later Lucas appeared, his cheeks a little bit red. They'd been caught. It was obvious from the look he gave Boone that his little brother wasn't happy that he'd had to leave the room and come back a little louder and more obvious.

"You ready to get that fence fixed?" Boone asked, happy to go along pretending nothing happened.

"I've been waiting on you."

"I'm heading that way now." Boone raised his hand but stopped himself. No, he wouldn't touch her cheek, or her arm. He wouldn't notice that mischievous gleam in her eyes. "I'm locking the doors. See that you keep them locked."

"Got it." She saluted.

He shook his head and headed out the back door with his brother. Lucas shot him a disgusted look as they walked the worn path to the barn.

"What?"

"What if Mom had walked in?" Lucas asked.

"This is the problem with being a grown man living too close to his family. I'm almost thirty, little brother. I think I can handle myself without your lectures. I don't think Mom would get too upset if she saw me," he said.

"If she saw you kissing Kayla in the kitchen?" Lucas shot him a knowing smirk. "Yeah, she'd be upset. Kayla is her little pet, big brother. Hurt Kayla and you'll be up a certain creek with no paddle."

"I'm not going to hurt her. I'm going to keep her safe and get her back to her life in Austin. End of story."

"These things never end well, Boone."

"There's nothing between us."

Lucas reached in the back of the old farm truck and pulled on a pair of leather gloves.

He shook his head and went back to digging for tools. "You're a fool."

Yeah, maybe he was. Maybe he'd started off on this job with all the right intentions and somewhere along the way he'd tripped up.

He pulled keys out of his pocket. "Get in the truck. We have fence to build."

Lucas was smart enough to choke back a laugh as he got in the truck. Boone shot him a warning look. By the time they finished building fence this evening, that laugh would be long gone. He'd make sure of it.

Chapter Eleven

It was close to sunset when Boone and Lucas showed up at the house. They stomped into the kitchen, dirty and looking worn out. Kayla sat by the patio doors reading a book but put it away to watch the two brothers. They scrambled to get to the sink, pushing each other away, then fighting over a towel. Boone gave Lucas a mild shove and told him to go take a shower.

"I will, because unlike you, I have a life." Lucas poured himself a glass of tea. "I have a date tonight."

"You're going to break Lily Martin's heart," Boone teased.

"She's thirteen!"

"Thirteen-year-old girls have hearts, too, you know," Kayla spoke up, reminding them that she was there. They glanced her way, Boone grinning and Lucas frowning.

Lucas wiped his face with the towel and hung it on the cabinet door. "Yeah, but I haven't done anything to make her feel this way."

"You exist. She's thirteen. Someday she'll understand that thirteen is a child compared to your what? Eighteen?"

"Nineteen, thank you very much. And Lily is a sweet kid. But she's still just a kid." He shot past them to the door, as if he couldn't get away soon enough. "You all have a great night. I heard the twins say they were going to a movie. Michaela was going to pick Molly up and go out with a friend. Who knows what Janie does?"

"Janie went to a small group meeting," Kayla offered. "I helped your mom fix soup and sandwiches for her and your dad."

"Sounds as if everyone is taken care of. See you all later." Then Lucas was gone. Leaving Boone and Kayla alone.

"I need to get cleaned up and get off my feet," he said as he sat down at the table with her. "How about we go to my place? I'll fix us something to eat. We can watch movies."

"You don't have to do that. I can heat a bowl of soup and just go to bed early."

He pushed himself to his feet. "Kayla, I know you didn't expect to live here for a month. But I'm not going to stop doing my job. You're not staying here alone."

No, she didn't think he would let her get away with that. But putting a little distance between them wouldn't be such a bad idea. Especially when he had that soft, vulnerable look around his eyes. It was a look that would make any woman cave.

"I'm not alone," she countered.

"Come on, we'll take my truck." He pulled out his keys and motioned for her to follow.

She wasn't winning this battle. But being with him felt dangerous. Almost as dangerous as whoever was stalking her. She shook off that thought. He wasn't a danger to her.

Only to her heart.

She'd never known anyone like him. Her world had been so shallow, filled with men who were useless, with relationships that went nowhere and experiences that left her empty and searching for more.

"Okay, we'll take your truck. Do you want me to drive?" she offered as they headed out.

In answer he tossed her his keys. "Go for it. Can you drive a standard?"

"A what?"

"Don't mess with me, Stanford. I'm too tired." But there was a light in his eyes, a glint of humor.

"Yes, Wilder, I can drive a standard," she assured him.

A few minutes later she climbed behind the wheel of his precious truck. It started and she eased off the clutch as she hit the gas. The vehicle lurched a little and Boone reached for the door.

"You said you could drive it."

She eased the truck forward, avoiding further lurching and bucking. "I didn't say I was any good at it. I just said I could drive it."

The truck jumped forward and died.

Boone leaned back in his seat. "Okay, put it in First."

She did.

"Start it with your foot on the clutch and the gas. Ease off the clutch. Ease. That means slowly."

She did as he told her. "I know what *ease* means."

He glanced her way, the look in his espresso-colored eyes warmed her heart.

"Stanford, you've never eased through anything. You rush into every situation full throttle."

"I believe in getting things done."

"I'm sure you do. Park close to the RV. I don't know if Daron will be home tonight."

"Home?" She took the keys out of the ignition. "Does he live here, too?"

He waited until they were climbing the steps to answer. "That depends on what you mean by *live*. I didn't ask for a roommate and he hasn't been invited to live here. He just shows up and sometimes forgets to leave."

His collie, Sally, hurried to his side, nudging against him as he unlocked the door. He pushed it open and the dog ran inside.

"Don't mind the mess. Daron thinks he's the neat one. He's not. And this place just isn't big enough for two. It's barely big enough for one."

"I like it," she responded.

Boone headed for the bedroom at the back of the RV. "I'll be back in a minute."

Kayla spotted the empty dog dish. She filled the water bowl and then dug around in cabinets until she found dog food to fill the other bowl. Sally gave her a suspicious look but accepted the food.

Boone returned a minute later, the left leg of his jeans pinned and crutches beneath his arms.

She stood there, unsure. "Are you okay?"

He grinned up at her. "Stanford, I'm okay. Fixing fence isn't exactly the easiest activity. But it's done."

"If you're sure." She wasn't. "I could make us some soup."

He stood. "Please don't. I'm fine. And I can fix us something a lot better than soup."

He glanced at the sink full of dishes. "Another Daron mess. Do you like omelets?"

"Do you have cheese?"

He opened the fridge door. "Yes, I have cheese."

"Then, I like omelets."

She ran water into the sink and watched as he cracked eggs into a bowl. He added peppers, mushrooms, ham and cheese. She leaned against the counter and watched.

"Do you want toast with this?" he asked as he poured the eggs into a pan. "The bread is in the cabinet. Butter is in the fridge. I think my mom put some of her homemade strawberry jam in there, too."

"Sounds perfect." She found the bread, and

then the butter and jam. "Your mom is an amazing woman."

He dropped bread into the four-slice toaster. "Yeah, she is. She's strong."

"She's raised strong kids."

"Yeah, she has. We're a wild bunch but our parents have managed to survive us. What about your family?"

Good question. "We're not close. Growing up, my dad spent most of his time at the office. It was always about the next case. My step-mother was busy climbing the social ladder as he climbed the career ladder. My brothers had their own lives."

"Sounds lonely," he observed.

"Yes, I guess it was. I thought it was typical. It was what I saw in so many of the families around us and so I didn't see it as dysfunctional."

"I guess you wouldn't if it was all you knew."

The toast popped up. She buttered it and spread jam. Boone lifted the pan and slid the omelet onto a plate. He cut it in half with the spatula and moved part of it to the second plate.

It was a strange, domestic moment in that tiny kitchen. They were close, too close. They were close physically and emotionally in ways she wasn't prepared for. As they brushed shoulders moving around the kitchen, she held her breath. Boone leaned his crutches against the counter and his hand touched her waist.

"You make it hard to breathe, Kayla." His voice was husky and close to her ear.

"Breathing is so overrated," she tried to joke.

"I've always found it to be pretty necessary to life." He slid his lips across her temple.

"The eggs will get cold."

"Yeah, that would be bad." He let go of her. "We should definitely eat."

She picked up the plates and carried them to the booth-style table. "I saw juice in the fridge. Do you want that or something else?"

He hopped to the fridge and pulled out the orange juice. "You?"

She nodded and took the juice from him. She poured two glasses. They sat down together at the table, Boone across from her. Sally sighed and stretched out on the floor. She looked up at them, her head resting on her paws.

"You know, you could press charges," Boone spoke as he polished off his eggs and toast.

"We have to know who it is before we press

charges, don't we? We can't just assume Jacobs is involved?"

"That isn't what I meant. Kayla, press charges against Whitman."

Her lungs were suddenly starved for oxygen and she blinked back tears welling in her eyes. It took her by surprise, those tears. She shook her head. He reached for her, grasping her fingers in his, grounding her.

"No one would believe me. It's been ten years."

"No statute of limitations for the assault of a child."

She pushed her plate away. The dog whined and stood, coming to rest her head on Kayla's leg. Absently she stroked Sally's head, looking into the animal's eyes.

"My dad would never forgive me. It's over. It was ten years ago."

Anger tightened Boone's mouth into a harsh line. "Kayla, what if there are other victims?"

"This isn't the conversation I want to have."

He stood, looking down at her, his features softening. "I'm sorry. You're right."

She followed him to the sink with their plates and when her hands were empty she reached for him, hugging him from the back, burying her face in his shirt. He didn't move.

He let her take that moment to find strength in him.

How in the world did he get himself in these situations? Good thing his cell phone came to his rescue. He stepped away from her and answered.

"Daron?" He leaned against the counter. And Kayla had put some breathing room between them.

"I have a few pictures I want Kayla to look at. The PI William Stanford hired has put the son of an ex-employee of her father and the nephew of the other senatorial candidate together."

"Okay." Boone glanced at Kayla. She'd started washing dishes, pretending she didn't care about the conversation. "When will you be here?"

"An hour," Daron told him.

"We'll be at my place." Boone sat down at the dining table.

"The two of you are there?" Daron said with a hint of amusement.

"Yeah, the two of us. See you in an hour. Drive safe."

Kayla sat down across from him. "They have something?"

"The son of an ex-employee of your dad.

He's friends with Ken Jacobs, Clarence Jacobs' nephew."

She buried her face in her hands and shook her head. "I don't know what I've done, Boone. I have blank spaces in my memory. I'm not proud of that. I'm not proud of who I've become."

"It isn't who you've become."

She looked up. "Really? Easy for you to say."

"It was a side trip. You aren't stuck there forever."

"I hope you're right."

"I'm right," he assured her. "We'll figure this out, get you safe and then you can go find the person you were meant to be."

Looking at her from across the table, the dim lighting of the RV leaving her face in shadows, he couldn't help but think that he'd miss her. He'd never missed a client. He'd liked a few. He'd worried about a couple.

He wasn't too worried about Kayla. She was strong. She would do something with her life. She'd probably have that career as a teacher. She'd get married and have kids. That thought took him down back roads that he shouldn't be going down, picturing her holding a pretty little girl in her arms with dark hair and blue eyes.

"I'm not sure who I'm meant to be, Boone." Her voice shook a little. "I've been on such a crazy journey in the past year and it seems as if it all led me here, to Martin's Crossing. I know I have to go home. Face the past. Figure out what to do in the future. But being here has meant everything."

"Then, you use it as a stepping-stone."

She nodded, resting her chin on her hands, her elbows propped on the table. "Your family has meant the world to me. I'm sorry that things started out so rough. I was difficult."

Now he laughed. "Difficult?"

Her mouth tilted on one side. "Yes, difficult."

He just stared at her.

"Okay, more than difficult. I didn't want a bodyguard. I didn't want to be thrust into the middle of your family, because I knew I wouldn't fit."

"You've done okay for yourself, Stanford."

"Thanks." She stood up. "Coffee?"

He started to stand. She put a hand on his shoulder.

"Let me," she said.

"Taking care of me, Stanford?"

"Yeah, Wilder. I guess I am. Don't tell anyone, but I'm going to miss you. And I'm going to hope I can become the type of woman that a man like you might love someday."

The words echoed between them. Her hand dropped from his shoulder and she stepped back. The distance she put between them was more than physical. There were things he could say, should say, to make her feel better.

But she was still a client. She was still looking for herself and her past. She was still the city girl who thought she didn't fit in their small town. He still had a bucket list that didn't include things like visiting Paris, but instead was all about taking care of his family.

"I can see you want to say something, Boone. Please don't. Don't reassure me or tell me what you think I want to hear. I know who I am and where I've been."

He reached for her hand and dragged it to his lips against his better judgment. Her eyes closed.

"I'm in over my head, Boone."

"Me, too."

"It's just the situation," she told him. "This is what happens when two people are thrown together in a dire situation. But we'll be fine. In a few months you'll be protecting someone else. I'll be working on that teaching certificate. We'll see each other at Duke's and we'll share stories about what we've been doing."

"Are we breaking up, Stanford?" He tried to keep his tone light.

"Don't be ridiculous. How could we break up? We're not a couple. I'm just saying, this isn't real. Every woman you ever protect is going to fall for you."

"Is that what's happening?"

She swallowed, then faked a smile. "Stop."

"Okay, but for the record, I don't have relationships with clients."

"Right. Silly me."

He stood, balancing, reaching for her. "There's nothing silly about this. Or about you."

She moved out of his reach. "I'm making coffee now."

The dog growled. Boone shot the animal a warning look. "Sally, it isn't an argument."

Sally stalked to the front door, the snarl coming from deep down in her chest. Boone flipped off the light and moved to the cabinet. He motioned for Kayla to get back. He doubted she'd listen, but maybe this once.

He unlocked the drawer and pulled out his weapon. Kayla's eyes widened and she shrank into the corner of the kitchen. Sally was at the door, her growl low and menacing. He might have thought it was Daron if the dog had just barked. But Sally reserved that special growl for intruders and varmints of the two-legged variety.

Boone moved forward. The doorknob jiggled. He hadn't locked it. Of course he hadn't. He never locked the door.

"Bathroom," he ordered in a whisper. He heard her scurry down the hall, heard the bathroom door close and lock.

The front door eased open. These people were idiots. They knew he was in here. They knew the lights had gone out after the dog growled. And they were still going to come in.

Boone slid against the wall and waited. He guessed they had him at a disadvantage. His prosthesis was on the other side of the room. His crutches were in the kitchen. But it didn't take much to see he had them outsmarted.

They were inside. He could see that they were young. What did they think they were going to do, take Kayla out of here? Over his dead body.

"You boys always go about breaking and entering? You know, out here in the country, we're usually packing." He said it low, and about as threatening as his dog's best growl. Sally had moved in next to him and that growl had gone way down deep in her chest. That was the growl that said she'd take the head off any varmint that crossed her.

"Dude," the kid started.

"Son, don't you *dude* me again. Put your hands up and we'll see that no one gets hurt."

"We're just going to take Kayla Stanford with us. We aren't going to hurt her." The taller of the two took a step forward.

Sally leaped, teeth bared. Both of them ran. Boone grabbed his crutches and did his best to catch up. He guessed they wouldn't be taking Kayla anywhere. But he also had hoped he'd be giving them a free ride to the county jail.

Headlights flashed up the drive. He hit Redial on his phone and Daron answered.

"They're heading through the east field. Two of them." He stayed on the porch. No way was he catching up with anyone.

"Stay with Kayla," Daron yelled as he jumped from his truck.

"Got it. I'll call County and have them head to the county road." Boone dialed 911 as he watched Daron take off through the field.

There was no moon. The countryside was dark. He gave information to the 911 dispatcher and then he stepped back inside the RV. Sally had gone with Daron.

"Kayla?" He flipped on lights as he headed down the hall. The bathroom door was still locked. "It's me. Open the door."

She was leaning against it. He could hear her breathing. He put a hand on the door and felt it shift.

"Open up."

"Give me a minute," she whispered.

"One minute and I'm coming in."

She opened the door. She didn't fall into his arms. She didn't touch him. She walked past him, down the hall to the living room. He followed, tossing the crutches in a corner and sitting next to her, but not touching her.

"I recognized his voice," she finally said.

"That coffee's done. Let me get us a cup."

She nodded. He got up and made his way to the kitchen. He poured two cups. When he turned she was standing next to him. She took one of the cups and poured in a few spoons of sugar.

This time she sat in the middle of the sofa. He sat next to her, their shoulders brushing. He stretched, rubbing the muscles of his left leg.

"You're okay?" she asked.

"Yeah, just muscle pains after a long day. You recognized his voice?"

She set her coffee on the table. "Yeah. After all this time, it took hearing the voice to jolt my memory. They were in Mexico. The night I crossed the border. They were younger than me. The senator's nephew hit on me. I'd forgotten. It wasn't one of my best nights. But I do remember telling him I wasn't interested. He tried to force the issue but a friend of his pulled him back, told him to go home to his mommy. He told me he'd make me sorry. It seems so silly now. It was just a stupid bonfire. He's a kid. Why would he do this?"

"Money and bruised ego."

"I guess."

The door opened. Daron walked in, gave the two of them a look, shook his head and made for the coffeepot. "They got away. But I got a description of the car."

"Kayla remembers them." Boone recounted what Kayla had shared with him. "It should be enough to at least bring them in. If the police get a search warrant, they might find some of the burn phones. And she recognized a voice."

"It was Ken Jacobs," Kayla explained.

Daron leaned against the counter with his cup. "Let's move this party to the main house.

These two aren't your garden-variety criminals. They aren't thinking. That makes them dumb and dangerous."

Boone pushed himself up from the sofa. "I've got to change and put things back together. The two of you go on to the house. And call Lucas. See if he's there. He can lock doors and make sure the girls are all accounted for."

"Boone, with that many sisters it's a wonder you sleep at night," Daron joked as he was pulling out his phone.

Kayla didn't move. "We can wait for you."

Of course she would say that. He grabbed his prosthesis and headed down the hall. It didn't take him long. New liner. New sock. He changed to tennis shoes because even he wasn't that attached to boots.

When he walked back to the living room in athletic shorts and tennis shoes, Kayla gave him a long look. She whistled.

"Not bad, cowboy."

"What does that mean?" He opened the door and stepped out on the porch, motioning her after him.

"I've always been a leg girl," she said.

"Well, I'm half the guy for you."

"You aren't half a man," she said.

Daron pushed past them. "Get in the truck. We know this isn't over."

Chapter Twelve

Kayla put on the coffee the next morning, then watched as Maria started cooking French toast. Sausage was already sizzling in a skillet.

"You're okay?" Maria asked. She handed over a fork. "I'm going to let you cook the sausage."

"I can do that."

It was just the two of them. Kayla knew she would miss these early mornings. She would definitely miss the Wilders.

Maria put the French toast on a baking sheet. "Well?"

"I'm good. It's been a crazy few weeks. I know it hasn't been easy for you, to have an extra person underfoot."

Maria waved off the comment. "Oh, honey, you're no trouble. We have so many kids in this house, what's one more? I'm only sorry that your time with us will come to an end soon."

"Me, too," she admitted. When she'd first come here, she never would have imagined this being the scenario at the end of her stay. "I've learned so much, Maria. Not just how to cook. But whatever faith I came here with, it's grown. I feel as if I can move forward. It's been a long time since I've felt this way."

Maria hugged her tight. "I'm so glad to hear you say that. I hope you know that our door is always open to you, Kayla. You've become a part of our family and I hope you'll visit. Often."

"Thank you." Kayla glanced at the clock on the stove. "The twins want to go shopping today. Their pageant is in six weeks and they're afraid I won't be around to help."

"Those girls. Don't let them push you into going if you don't want to go."

Boone limped into the kitchen and leaned heavily on the counter. "Oh, don't worry. It isn't Kayla who's being pushed into going shopping."

Maria patted his cheek. "Poor Boonie."

Kayla raised her brows at the nickname. "Boonie?"

"Only my mom gets to call me that." He

poured himself a cup of coffee. "Don't burn the sausage, Stanford."

She turned the sausage. "I won't. *Boonie*."

"Thanks, Mom." He headed for a stool and sat to watch them finish breakfast.

"You should tell the girls it isn't a good day," his mom said. "They'd understand."

"This is important to them."

"Yes, it is. But it isn't more important than your life."

"I think we can go without you," Kayla offered.

"Nice try." Boone winked as he lifted his cup of coffee to his lips. "We leave in an hour."

A few hours later they were walking through the mall. Essie and Allie were all energy and no focus. Essie, sometimes a little quieter than her sister, Kayla thought, tried to calm her twin. Boone followed them, watchful and attentive.

"We need a plan." Kayla had never been in a pageant, so she had no idea what that plan would be.

The girls started to talk at the same time. Kayla opened her mouth, unable to get a word in.

"Okay, girls, listen to Kayla." Boone grabbed both twins by the arms just as they were about to hare off to a shoe store. "Because I'm not going in every single store in this mall."

"You need evening gowns, right? And jewelry."

"Yes." Allie, the blue jeans, cowboy boots and T-shirt twin, was all giddy at the mention of jewelry.

"This way." Kayla motioned for them to follow. She glanced back at Boone. "You got this?"

"I've got this." He gave her a tight grimace that she thought was meant to be a smile.

"Of course you do." Overnight she'd told herself that she'd be leaving soon and he'd be nothing but a bright moment in her life, sweet but in the past.

And she didn't want him to hurt.

"Keep walking, Stanford. I'm good."

She reached for his hand. "I'll walk with you."

"You're only encouraging them," he grumbled.

"I don't think they need any encouragement."

He pulled her a little bit closer to his side. "Yeah, and neither do I."

The shop they entered sparkled with lights,

gowns of all colors and sizes and costume jewelry. Boone shuddered a little.

"This is the kind of store that gives a man hives," he said.

"And you act so tough. There's a bench inside. For men forced to shop with sisters."

"I'll be here at the door. I would say to take your time but I'm afraid you will."

"I'll try to hurry them," she offered. "And you're not okay."

"No, I'm not. But today isn't the day to worry about it. I'll get it taken care of tomorrow."

"Tomorrow is the ranch rodeo."

"It is. Just shop and let me do my job."

She nodded and backed away, from him and from what she was feeling.

Allie waited for her midway through the store. She had a gown of deep burgundy held up against her. "What do you think?"

"Gorgeous. Perfect color. You should try it on."

Allie looked down at the gown. "Really? I don't know. We have a budget. We've saved for this, but we can't go crazy."

"Try it on." Kayla pulled a similar gown, same color but a little different design, off the rack. "And your sister should try this one."

Essie suddenly appeared. She took the dress and held it up. "It's beautiful, but I don't know."

"Try them on."

She watched them go into the dressing rooms, then she stopped at the register, where she handed over her credit card. "I'm paying."

Because this family had done so much for her. They'd shared their love and their faith with her. She wanted to give back.

Allie came out, the dress soft and shimmering. "It's gorgeous, but we can't. If we could find something similar but less expensive."

"Allie, get the dress. It's beautiful. And I've found jewelry that will look beautiful with it. I want to do this for you."

"Mom would never let us accept it," Essie said as she walked out of the dressing room.

"It's a gift," Kayla insisted. "Come on. We can't keep your brother standing out there much longer."

Essie shot a concerned look at Boone, standing at the entrance of the store. "I think he must have pressure sores. It hasn't happened in a long time. But the weather is changing and he's been going nonstop."

"What does he need to do when this happens?" Kayla asked as she followed them into the dressing room area and stood outside the rooms where they were changing.

"He needs to go in and get checked. But he needs to stay off it, and probably not wear the prosthesis for a few days."

They were paying when Boone left his post at the door and hurried toward them. He was on the phone, his mouth a grim line. Kayla stepped away from Essie and Allie. They were busy telling the cashier all about the twin pageant.

"What's wrong?" she asked.

"Dad. They think he's having another heart attack. Jase is driving him to the Braswell hospital."

"Let's go." She signed for their purchases, ignoring the look Boone gave her. "Come on, girls, time to head out."

"What's up?" Essie asked as she and Allie moved to Boone's side.

"Your dad is having chest pains," Kayla explained. "We're going to meet them at Braswell."

Allie slipped her arm through Boone's. "He's okay, isn't he?"

"Of course he is," Boone reassured his younger sisters. "He's fine. He was talking. Jase is there."

Kayla gave the three of them space. Boone noticed. "Stanford, I'm still paying attention. Come here."

"I can't catch a break with you." She moved ahead of the three, leading them through the crowded mall, mindful of Boone's lagging pace. They had a long walk to get to the parking lot.

She hurried ahead of them, ignoring Boone when he told her to stay with him. She grabbed a wheelchair, paid the fee and headed in his direction. He shook his head.

Essie pushed him toward the chair. "Get in, big brother. You're slowing us down."

"I'm the bodyguard," he mumbled.

"And you're guarding us. But you can't do it if you end up in the hospital." Allie kissed his cheek. "Don't worry, you're still tough. No one will argue with that."

Kayla ignored the look he gave her. She grabbed the handles and pushed. He yanked off his cowboy hat and looked back at her.

"This isn't necessary," he grumbled.

"It is. You're in pain. Your sisters say the longer you walk like this, the more damage you can do. And we're in a hurry."

She expected him to be upset but he reached back and touched her hand. The gesture undid her but she kept moving forward. She wondered what he'd do if she stopped in the middle of the mall and kissed him. Because she really wanted to. She wanted to kiss him until she was breathless. She wanted promises from him.

And she'd never wanted that from anyone else.

Boone led his sisters and Kayla through the Braswell Doctors Hospital. His dad had been put in the cardiac unit. As they were heading out of Austin, Jase had called to let him know it had been a mild heart attack, but they were keeping Jesse Wilder at least overnight.

His mom met them as they were coming down the hall. She looked pale. And tired. He didn't like that everything had been piled on her shoulders while he'd been in Afghanistan, and then while he'd been recuperating. All that he'd done in the past couple of years had been to make things a little easier for her, and for his father.

"He's going to be fine," she told them. She squeezed his hand and then hugged his sisters. She didn't exclude Kayla, pulling her close.

The hug Kayla gave in return was one of

comfort. For his mom. She was a giver, Kayla was. She just hadn't realized it before.

"Of course he's going to be fine," Kayla assured his mom. "Have you eaten?"

"I couldn't."

"I'll get you something. If there's a cafeteria. Or I can take Boone's truck. I'll bring something back for all of you."

"Stanford," Boone warned. She gave him an innocent look. "You're not going anywhere alone."

"I'll be fine," she assured him. Her arm was still around his mom.

"Don't worry about me. Go in and see your dad," Maria encouraged. "He was worried. He knows Lucas is looking forward to the rodeo tomorrow. And he doesn't want you distracted from your job."

"Those are two things he doesn't need to worry about," Boone told his mom.

The twins had already gone into their dad's hospital room. He could see that all of his siblings were gathered inside, making the room crowded.

"Go on in. I'll go see if Samantha is working," Kayla said, walking away from his mom.

"Stay inside. And keep your phone with you."

"Will do, Wilder," she answered.

She pulled her phone from her pocket as she left. Boone's mom touched his arm. He managed a quick smile and then he led her into his dad's room. Jesse looked up, his smile weak, but he wasn't as pale as he'd seemed for the past week or so.

"You know, Dad, you could have all of this attention at home. You don't have to come here."

His dad's mouth twisted in a crooked grin. "I didn't plan on it being a family reunion."

"No, I bet you didn't. How are you?"

His dad rubbed his chest. "Better. How are you?"

"I'm good, Dad."

"We're not going to miss that rodeo tomorrow."

"Dad, that's the last thing we need to be worrying about," Boone said as he moved closer to the bed.

"No, it's the one thing to worry about. This rodeo means a lot to Lucas. To all of you."

"Yeah, so does your health. And this won't be the last rodeo."

"No, I guess it won't. But if there's a way, I want you all in it."

For Lucas. Boone got that. "I know."

Jesse reached for his wife's hand. "Take your mom down and make her eat."

"I'll try."

"Jesse, I'm not hungry," Maria assured her husband, softening the words with a kiss on his cheek. "The kids went down to eat. Jase brought me back a salad."

Boone made eye contact with his brother. Jase shook his head.

"I want you to take care of yourself, Maria." Jesse patted his wife's hand.

Boone pulled up a chair for his mom. "Sit. I'm going to find Kayla and we'll bring you back something to eat."

"I could go," Michaela offered. He noticed she was alone.

"Where's Molly?"

"With Breezy Martin. She's fine. I'm going to head that way soon. Essie and Allie can go with me. Janie is going to stay here tonight. With Mom."

Boone's gaze landed on Janie. She was sitting near the window, a book in her hand. She always had a book. Sometimes he worried that she lived her life through fiction and avoided real life.

He didn't know how to help her. For that matter, how did he help Michaela move on from her divorce? How did he help the twins to stay grounded, and Lucas to feel as if he wasn't the son who had been skipped over?

His mom was still standing. He glared at her, pointing to the chair.

She sat down but she gave him a look that he knew well. The one that said he was trying her patience. He leaned down to kiss her cheek, softening her mood the way he'd always done. He'd been told he'd been doing it since he was a little boy. If he tried her patience, he knew it just took a hug, a kiss on the cheek and she melted.

"I'll be back."

"We'll be fine," she assured him.

He left, stepping into the hall. Out of eyeshot from the others, he leaned against the wall and took a deep breath. He let it out slowly, letting the pain go with it.

"Hey, cowboy, having problems?" Samantha had walked up, taking him by surprise. Kayla wasn't with her.

"Where's your sister?"

"You're so charming," she teased. "She went to get your mom something to eat. But first she came to find me because she said you're stubborn."

"I'm just fine." He took a step, pretending it didn't hurt.

"Yeah, she told me you'd try to deny it. And she was right. Come upstairs. We have a doctor on duty and he said he'd look at it. We want to make sure you don't have an infection. I'll get you crutches to use and you can give it a rest for a day or two."

"Sam, I don't have time for resting."

She took hold of his arm and led him to the elevator. "You also don't have time to be in pain. Come on."

An hour later he was on crutches and heading back down to his dad's room. Kayla met him in the hall.

"Samantha found you?" She smiled as she asked.

"Yes, she found me." He motioned her toward a waiting room. "Sit with me."

"Is this going to be serious? Are we breaking up?" she teased.

"Kayla." He didn't know what else to say. She was joking. He knew it was her way of hiding from the pain.

"Okay, so this *is* that moment. It's been fun. We'll see each other from time to time."

He kept walking and she followed, still talking about how life would be when she left. He opened the door of the waiting room and she entered ahead of him. He was relieved to see the room empty.

She sat and he took a seat across from her.

"So?" She looked up, her blue eyes a little misty.

"Daron is coming to get you. If I can get Mom to leave, he said he'd drive her back to the ranch, too. He's going to stay with you all tonight so I can stay here."

"I see. And then?"

"Your dad is coming to see you tomorrow. I think he wants to take you back to Austin. They feel sure they're going to have these guys in custody in the next few days."

"So it's really over."

"Almost. You can go back to your life."

She gave him a thoughtful look. "No, I don't think so. Not the life I've been living. The past year or so has been a journey and I think it's brought me to this place, to a new understanding of myself. I'm not going back to that, I'm going forward."

"I'm glad, because you deserve more than you've allowed yourself to have."

"I do, don't I?" Her smile was genuine now. "Thank you, Boone. Your family has meant a lot to me."

The words were all making sense. This was what they were supposed to say. *It's been nice. Things will be better.* But the words weren't right.

Nothing about this moment felt right. Boone stood, because he didn't know what else to say, other than goodbye.

Chapter Thirteen

William Stanford showed up in Martin's Crossing Saturday morning. The limousine was black with tinted windows. His bodyguards didn't wear cowboy boots. Kayla stood on the front porch of the Wilder home, uncertain and a little uneasy. Her dad walked up the steps and pulled her into a hug.

"Dad."

"Kayla, I'm glad you're okay."

The words seemed genuine. "Of course I'm fine."

"We should talk," he continued. "Is there somewhere we can go?"

"There's a bench out by the barn, if that's okay."

They walked, not talking, not touching. It had been a long time since they'd been close. Hugs were in the past, in her child-hood. Shared secrets had never been a part of their relationship. He'd been busy. She'd been angry.

She hadn't forgiven him because she hadn't wanted to give him that gift. But now she saw that forgiving was for her, to give her the ability to let go.

"I forgive you," she said as they sat down on the bench.

He looked surprised.

"You let me down and you didn't protect me. I've been angry with you for a long time. I was hurt. I felt betrayed. I felt as if I had no one."

He adjusted his tie, something he'd always done when he wasn't sure what to say. She waited, because the next words had to come from him. She was out of words. She needed his.

"You're right," he finally said. "I fired Jim. We met last night and I told him he was no longer needed. I also asked him to leave the law firm."

A year ago she would have told him too lit-tle, too late. Today she took his hand and gave it a light squeeze.

"Thank you." She drew in a breath. "Dad, I

have to go to the police. About Paul. I'm sorry. I know it will hurt your campaign. I don't want to do that, but I can't let him hurt anyone else."

There was a long silence between them. She braved a look at her dad. He was clenching his jaw. His gaze was on the field, on cattle grazing.

"You're right," he finally said. "I don't want scandal. But it isn't scandal. It's justice."

Her heart thumped hard, working through the fear. Ten years. She'd been fighting and she'd been alone for ten years. She wanted to hug her dad, to pretend those ten years hadn't happened. It seemed that even with forgiveness, even with his apology, she still had a lot to work through.

"I'm not going back to Austin," she told him. "I will someday. I just can't go back today. Or this week. I need to stay here and help the Wilders. They've opened their home and their lives to me. I want to give back a little of what they've given."

"I don't understand."

"Boone's dad…" She paused. "Mr. Wilder had a heart attack. I don't want to leave until he's well and back home."

"I understand that they've been good to you, Kayla. But I think it's time for you to come home. There's going to be a lot of damage control that needs to be done in the coming weeks before the election."

"I understand, but my life is about more than your political campaign, Dad. For years I haven't really been a part of your life or your family. I get it. You didn't expect a child from your relationship with Sylvia. You certainly didn't expect me to be dumped on you. But I'm tired of not really being a part of your life." Her hands trembled and she clasped them together.

"You're my daughter," her dad finally said. "I'm sorry if you felt anything other than loved."

"Thank you."

He stood, tall and imposing. She got up, facing him, almost as tall and every bit as proud. He gave a curt nod. "One week."

"Thank you. And when I come home, I'm going to do what you need me to do. I'll attend your campaign events. I'll avoid trouble."

A hint of a smile tugged at his mouth. "I'm not sure you can do that."

"I'm not, either, but I'm going to try my best."

They walked back to the house. Not arm in arm. It was too soon for that. But they were on the mend, she thought. And maybe the healing would spread to the rest of their family. She thought of her little brother, Michael. They'd never been close. Maybe they could find a way to at least be friends.

After her dad left, she went inside to find the twins. They were sprawled on their beds looking at fashion magazines. When she entered their room, they looked up, clearly surprised to see her.

"Weren't you leaving?" Essie rolled over and sat up.

"I'm staying. Your mom is going to need help here." She shrugged. Did she really think she could help Maria Wilder?

"Boone is going to be surprised." Allie was still looking at a magazine. "So what do you plan on doing?"

"I thought we should clean the house. And maybe start dinner."

Essie tossed her magazine on the bed. "Seriously?"

"Yes, seriously. We can start soup for dinner."

Allie put aside her magazine and sat up. "Do you know how to make soup?"

"Allie, I have a smartphone. I can do anything."

Two hours later they were in the kitchen

together, rummaging through cabinets, positive they had made the best gumbo in history. Allie took a taste with a spoon.

"It's spicy," she said. "But a good kind of spicy. Not the kind that makes your eyeballs sweat."

"Sweaty eyeballs?" Daron walked into the room. "That sounds appetizing."

"We made gumbo," Allie informed him. She held out the spoon. "Try it."

"Hey, not bad."

Suddenly there was a commotion at the front of the house. Voices. Footsteps.

"They're home," Allie called out as she hurried from the room. Essie followed.

Kayla remained in the kitchen. Daron had taken a seat and he shot her a look, one brow arched. She gave the look right back.

"I thought you'd be glad to head back to the city."

"I will be. But I wanted to repay Maria. She's been wonderful to me. And she's going to need some help around here."

"She has four daughters."

"I'm aware of that, Daron. But I wanted to do something for them."

He held up his hands in surrender. "Gotcha."

She turned the flame under the soup down. "Maybe I should have left."

"No, you shouldn't have left. They'll be glad you're here. And I'm sure if you keep cooking like that, you will make things easier for everyone."

The family returned to the kitchen. Essie and Allie were practically pulling Maria. Boone helped his dad to walk, holding his arm and guiding him to a chair. Michaela and Janie followed.

Jase and Lucas had been home all day. They were moving forward with their plans for the rodeo. Jesse had insisted that his sons still participate.

Daron got up, giving his seat to Michaela, who held a sleeping Molly. Kayla watched from the corner of the kitchen. She had the gumbo simmering and the rolls in the oven baking. Essie began to make lemonade.

She should leave and let the family be alone. She started to tell Allie that the soup was done and that the rolls would have to be taken out in five minutes. Boone moved to her side, preventing her from escaping.

"You've been busy," he said in a quiet voice.

"I wanted to be here to help," she explained.

He caught her gaze, holding it, that half tilt of his mouth distracting her.

"That's good of you. But you should have gone back with your dad."

She managed an easy smile. "Trying to get rid of me, Wilder?"

"No, just trying to keep you safe and help you find your way back to your life. What if you get stuck here in the country, making casseroles and cleaning bathrooms?"

"There are worse things."

He pushed his hat back on his head and leaned against the counter. "For what it's worth, I know my mom appreciates you being here."

She waited, wanting him to say more. But he didn't. They were from different worlds and this had all been temporary. All of it. Her time with the Wilders, and her time in his life.

Bright lights illuminated the Martin's Crossing Saddle Club arena. The stands were packed. The adjacent field was crowded with horse trailers and pickups. Boone backed his gelding out of the trailer. Lucas already had his horse out, saddled, and was warming up in the open area next to the arena.

He didn't want to be here. Not tonight. But

his dad had insisted. They were doing this for Lucas. Boone, Jase, Lucas and Janie were riding for Team Wilder. Michaela was in the stands with the twins and Molly.

Kayla was standing next to the truck. His mom had insisted she attend, even though she'd wanted to stay home with his parents. He slid his gaze her way but didn't linger there too long. She was leaning against the truck, in jeans, pigtails and Michaela's hand-me-down boots. He knew she could afford a pair of her own. She probably had a half dozen pairs in that fancy apartment of hers in Austin.

But she liked those worn boots of his sister's.

He led his horse to the side of the trailer and tied him up. Kayla settled on the wheel well of the trailer to watch.

"You're still limping," she said, her tone casual.

"Yep."

"Should you be doing this?"

He pulled a saddle out of the tack compartment of the trailer. "Yeah, I should. There are times you have to do what needs to be done, Kayla."

"I know."

He placed the blanket on his horse's back

and then the saddle. She continued to watch. He tightened the cinch, adjusted the stirrups and then gave the cinch another tug to make sure it was snug.

"What events are you entered in?"

"Branding," he started.

"For real?" she asked, her eyes widening.

He grinned at that look. "Not for real. There will be a pen of calves. We'll rope them by number and bring them to the branding area and mark them with chalk."

"Okay, and then what?"

"Steer doctoring and team penning."

"And at the end of the night, if he wins, he gets to dance with the girl of his choice."

He turned, wishing for once that Remington Jenkins wasn't back in the area. In a matter of weeks he would be Kayla's brother-in-law. He and Samantha Martin were getting married.

"I don't think there's a dance." Boone slid the bridle over his horse's head. "Who do you have on the Jenkins team, Remington?"

"Ah, but there is a dance. The Carter Brothers are playing after the event and they've set up a dance floor," Kayla said.

Boone ignored Kayla. "Your team?"

"Myself, Sam, my brother Colt and Bryan Cooper. He's Breezy's… I don't know, I guess he's nothing to Breezy. But her biological sister is a Cooper, adopted by them years ago. Bryan is her brother by adoption?"

"Confusing," Boone said. "But I've met him. Good guy. Spent some time in South America on the mission field?"

"That's the one. The Coopers are a big family, from northeast Oklahoma." Remington turned his attention to Kayla. "So, little sister, aren't you riding?"

"I don't think anyone wants that," she said with a quick laugh. "The goal here is to win, isn't it?"

Remington laughed and pushed back his hat. "Yes, I guess it is. Give it time. You can't hang with this crowd for long and not be a part of things like this."

"Maybe someday," she answered.

Boone settled his gaze on her. He could see it happening. When those boots felt as if they belonged on her feet and the jeans were worn from ranch work and not by a trick of manufacturing.

"I'd best get back to my crew." Remington tipped his hat. "I'm sure we'll see you at church tomorrow."

From the arena, the MC announced the first event. Calf branding. Boone untied his horse.

"Walk with me?" he offered to the woman standing by his truck looking a little unsure, as if she'd suddenly realized she didn't belong here.

She nodded and walked alongside. His big chestnut moved in too close, nudging him. Cin, short for Cinnamon. The horse had the worst name around.

The quiet between them didn't feel settled or peaceful. He wasn't sure what to do about it, how to fix it. Or even if he should. Maybe it was better this way. To everything there is a season, his mom had always told them, people came and went. There were seasons even for friendships, she'd told them as kids, when a friend moved, a breakup resulted in a broken heart, when they'd lost grandparents.

This had been Kayla Stanford's season in their lives. He had thought it had been mostly for her, to help her face her life. But today he'd seen things in a different light. She'd grown up, and been there for his family.

"I'm going to leave Monday," she said as they approached his family. Janie was on her horse. Jase and Lucas were messing with Lucas's mare, picking her front hoof. She'd probably picked up a stone.

"It isn't goodbye," he said to the woman at his side.

She looked up at him, the borrowed cowboy hat leaving her face in shadows. He moved the brim of that hat, giving him a better view of her face, her eyes. He considered kissing her, but the good sense he'd been born with prevailed. This wasn't the time or the place.

"I know it isn't," she responded. "I'll be around. I'd like to think we've become friends. Even if you were against babysitting me back when this all started."

"We're friends," he assured her.

She stood on tiptoe and kissed his cheek. "Go beat those Martins."

He moved to the right side of his horse, definitely the off side for mounting. But he and Cin had gotten used to it. He swung into the saddle, settling in the seat and steadying the horse, which shifted beneath him.

"Don't worry, we'll teach 'em how it's done." He tipped his hat and she laughed.

Lucas moved his horse around to Boone's left. The four of them rode toward the gate. Kayla went off to sit with her family. Breezy, Oregon, Lily and the younger children. He glanced her way one last time.

Sometime during the branding of their third calf, he looked up again and realized she was gone.

Chapter Fourteen

Kayla's phone had buzzed. When she looked down, the text glared up at her, making her blood run cold. But she'd managed to smile and pretend everything was fine. She told Breezy she was a little cool and was going to grab her jacket out of Boone's truck. Instead, she'd gotten behind the wheel of the truck and guided it out of the parking lot, careful to ease off the clutch, conscious of the large stock trailer on the back.

Her phone buzzed a second time. They wanted to know if she was coming. Alone.

She texted that she was.

She drove out of the rodeo grounds and onto the highway, the trailer jerking the truck, making it a little harder for her to ease forward the way Boone had taught her. It would take her at least ten minutes to get back to the Wilders. She texted again, telling the person on the other end to be patient. She was coming. She'd do whatever they said.

A smiley face was the response. Daron had been right. These guys were young and dangerous. She kept driving, the truck feeling heavy with the trailer on the back. Or maybe it was her, feeling weighted down, as if she couldn't move fast enough.

The slower speed gave her time to think, time to plan. But she didn't have a plan. She only knew that she wouldn't let anyone hurt Maria or Jesse Wilder.

She pulled up to the farmhouse. The place looked sleepy and innocent, as if there couldn't possibly be anyone here threatening her or the family that had been so good to her. She got out of the truck and closed the door quietly, hoping she could make a circle of the house and see if she saw anyone. She remembered that Boone had a gun in his RV. The door would be unlocked.

She took a dozen steps and someone grabbed her.

"Don't move. Don't say a word."

She nodded.

"I've been waiting for this day for a long

time. You thought you were too good for me, didn't you, Kayla Stanford? You told me I was a stupid kid. But look who is going to win."

"I can't look. You're behind me."

"You don't need to see me. I'm so unimportant to you, you didn't even think that I might be the one pulling the strings, making you and your daddy dance. But I'm going to show you. I've sent the article to the paper. Tomorrow morning everyone will know about Paul Whitman."

"He's no longer working for my father," she countered.

"I don't really care about him. I care about you. I care about your father's money. He fired my father. No explanation, just told him he wasn't needed any longer. Because of that my father started drinking and never stopped. He died last year."

"I'm sorry." No one should live like that. Or die like that. "Blane. That's your name, right? Where's Ken?"

Hadn't she read somewhere that if you make a personal connection with an attacker, it softens them? She glanced around looking for the other man and didn't see him.

"Don't worry about where Ken is and don't try to act as if we're friends."

"Are the Wilders okay?" she asked, desperate enough to continue trying the friendship tactic.

"They're fine. We tied them up. They haven't done anything to us. We just wanted you."

"Okay, you have me. Where are we going? Where's your friend?"

"He's getting the car. We parked on the side road."

"What are you going to do with me?" She glanced around, hoping to see an escape route. She saw Sally, Boone's collie. The dog was easing out of the shadows, the snarl low in her chest. He didn't hear the dog.

"Ransom," he said. "We figure you're worth enough to get us out of the country. But first, we'll have some fun."

"Good. I do like a decent party."

In the distance she heard a car. His friend maybe. Sally came closer, her growl a little louder.

"I'm about sick of that dog." He pulled a gun. She elbowed him in the face as he took aim at the collie. The bullet went wide. The gun flew from his hand. A car came up the driveway.

She broke loose and ran. She wouldn't go

to the house. She couldn't put Boone's parents at risk. Instead, she ran for the RV. Inside it was dark and quiet. She locked the doors and leaned against the paneled wall, waiting for her heart to return to normal.

Blue lights flashed across the walls of the camper. Outside she heard Sally give one sharp bark, asking for the door to be opened. Kayla unlocked the door and let the dog in. And in the dark she saw a shadow, and then a figure emerged.

"It's me." Boone stepped forward, limping up the steps of the camper. "You're okay?"

She nodded, unable to speak.

He took off his hat and tossed it on the patio table. "Kayla, I..."

"I didn't want them to hurt your parents."

He brushed a hand down his face. "I'm so mad at you, I don't know what to say. You could have gotten yourself killed."

"But I didn't."

"No, you didn't." He shook his head. "I can't think straight right now. But your father is on his way. He's taking you back to Austin, because I can't have you here if I can't keep you safe."

"But you got them."

"Yeah, I got them. But right now you're not

safe from me. I don't know if I want to throttle you or kiss you."

"Kiss me?" she suggested.

He shook his head. "Come on, my mom wants to see with her own two eyes that you're safe."

She reached for his hand. He wouldn't take it.

"Not right now," he said. "You should have trusted me."

"I know. But I didn't want anyone to get hurt on my account. I wanted to protect you all."

"I do the protecting around here. I don't need you to protect me."

"No, you don't." She walked next to him back to the house.

"Your brothers and sister are here." He nodded, indicating the yard full of trucks.

"Great."

"You have a lot of explaining to do."

"They said to come alone," she tried to explain.

He shook his head. "You have us for a reason. You don't have to do things alone anymore. You especially don't have to give in to the demands of blackmailers."

"They said the story is going to be in the paper tomorrow."

He stopped her, his hand on her arm. "Maybe it is. Maybe it isn't. But you're going to survive that. Your father will survive it. You have to trust the people in your life."

"I know."

Then she was surrounded by family. Boone walked away, leaving her to her siblings. Jake took control, telling her to get her bag. Her father could pick her up at the Circle M Ranch.

She allowed Jake to walk her out the door and down to his truck without a goodbye to Boone.

She took the handkerchief he offered as they drove away. Somehow she would come out of this stronger than ever. She knew that. Someday soon she would thank Boone for giving her the opportunity to find herself.

But today was not that day.

Boone woke up to early-morning sunshine filtering through the miniblinds. He rolled over and almost fell off the narrow sofa of his RV. Sally whimpered and scrambled to stay on the cushion. He glanced down at her.

"What are you doing on the couch?"

In response she slid off and curled up on the floor.

"You going to sleep all day?"

He jumped at the familiar voice. "What are you doing here?"

Daron was stretched out in the recliner.

"I thought you might need backup. By the time I got here, everyone was gone or asleep. You didn't hear me come in."

"I'm going to change the locks."

"You won't do that. You'd miss me."

"I wouldn't." Boone sat up, stretched and reached for his crutches. "I've got a doctor's appointment this morning."

"Yeah, I heard. Want me to drive you?"

"If you would. Have you talked to Lucy?"

"Yeah, she's good. She's in San Angelo on a job."

"Gotcha. Have you talked to Mr. Stanford today?"

Daron headed for the kitchen and started the coffeemaker. "Yeah, he's glad this is over. The article did come out. It made him look bad, but the real criminal is Mr. Whitman. Kayla is going to press charges. I guess you didn't think you could tell me about that."

"No, I didn't. She told me in confidence."

"She doesn't confide in a lot of people," Daron said as he leaned against the counter.

Boone opened the fridge. He pulled out a package of sausage and found a clean skillet.

"You could do the dishes today," he told Daron.

"Yeah, I will. Or hire someone. Do you think the twins would want to earn extra money?"

Boone put the pan on the burner. "The twins always want extra money. But I'm not going to pay them to clean the RV."

"Then, I will. About Kayla. She's going to be okay. I think she'll be better than ever. It's you I'm not so sure about."

"I'm fine." Boone poured the coffee that had brewed into his cup. He lifted the cup to salute Daron.

"I don't think you're fine, Boone. I think you got too close."

"You're not the head of this organization, Daron. We're partners. You're definitely not my boss or my mom. I don't need your advice."

"No, but you do need your head on straight for the next job."

"My head is on straight."

Daron grabbed a spatula and flipped the

sausage. "You're right. I'm out of line. What time is your doctor's appointment?"

"Ten."

"So do you love her?"

Boone stilled, then pointed at the door. "Get out."

"Listen, if you need to talk…"

"I'll get a therapist if I need to talk."

"Boone, it wasn't your fault. The kid, he had us all fooled."

"The kid was a pawn." Boone said the words clearly, not allowing emotion to get the best of him. "And why do you think everything goes back to that day?"

"Because it does. We all relive it every day."

"Do you?" Boone leaned against the counter and watched his friend fry sausage until it no longer resembled food.

"Yeah, I do. I convinced James he should go with us. I'm not sure what we thought we were going to do."

"We thought we would check it out and then go back with a plan to extract those guys."

"But they were waiting for us," Daron said.

Boone looked away. He didn't want to see the nightmare relived on his friend's face. He didn't want Daron to see it on his. They couldn't talk about that day without experiencing it all over again. The explosion. The heat. The screams. The pain.

"We made a stupid pact, while you were in the hospital." Daron turned off the pan. "Protect others. Live our lives for the brother we lost. We were a lot younger then."

"We were young." They'd been twenty-five. Not really that young, he guessed. But young enough to think they needed a pact to honor their fallen friends. If James wasn't going home to his family, Daron and Boone would never have families. Except that Daron had promised James he'd keep an eye on Emma and Jamie.

"If you love her, you should go for it, Boone. Don't let her get away."

Daron handed him a plate with a few burned sausages.

"I'm not sure what I feel." Boone sat down at the table. Daron sat across from him. "You know the emotions in situations like this aren't always real."

"Yeah, you're right, not always. It's a job and we can get caught up in some stuff. But you've always kept your emotions separate from the job. This time you didn't."

"No, this time I didn't. She took me by surprise, Daron. I didn't expect her. I didn't expect to feel this way."

"Don't let her get away," Daron said off-handedly as he stood and dumped sausage in the dog's dish. "I'm going to Duke's for breakfast."

"Good idea."

Don't let her get away. He brushed off the advice. They couldn't build a relationship on what they felt in the middle of a crisis situation. Kayla had depended on him to keep her safe. He'd felt like the man rescuing her from danger and from herself.

In time they'd come back to earth and see the relationship for what it was. Temporary. And if he missed her for a little while, that was normal.

They'd felt a bond only because he was her bodyguard and he had liked playing the hero.

They just needed time to realize that their relationship had been built on close proximity and the situation they'd been in.

But in truth, he couldn't imagine a time when he wouldn't think about her. What was he going to do about that?

Chapter Fifteen

Kayla stood next to her father when he was sworn in as Texas state senator. The next day she left for Martin's Crossing.

Samantha and Remington were getting married at the end of the week. Kayla wouldn't miss that wedding for the world. She pulled up to her sister's small house and for a moment sat in the truck she'd recently traded her car for. Samantha walked out the front door, waved and then headed her way.

"Well, look what the cat dragged in." Sam leaned in the window and kissed her on the cheek. "I'm glad to see you. I need help packing."

After the honeymoon Sam would be moving to the Jenkins ranch. Kayla had asked to stay in this house on the Martins' property.

She was going to apply for a job at the Martin's Crossing Consolidated School. She was going to live in the country. She'd already sold her condo. She'd traded off her convertible. She had a pair of boots that were meant for the farm, not the club.

She would see Boone. Often. Her heart beat faster on that thought.

"I'll do whatever you need me to do," she assured Sam as she climbed down from the truck.

"I'm glad to hear that. I've got so much to get done. And tonight is the family dinner at Duke's. So you're just in time."

"I'm not sure I'm ready to go to town," Kayla admitted as they crossed to the little cottage that she'd come to love.

She immediately plopped on the oversize sofa and grabbed her favorite afghan. It felt so good to be home. She smiled up at her sister, and for a minute she forgot her loneliness, the emptiness that sometimes caught her by surprise.

"Why?" Sam moved a box and sat on the chair, pulling it close to the sofa so she could put her feet on the coffee table.

"Because I'm not ready."

"You're going to see him eventually. And you know that you want to see him."

"I know. But it shouldn't be so hard. It was a month of my life. Barely. It wasn't exactly a relationship that we broke off. I shouldn't..." She sighed.

"Miss him?" Sam gave her a sweet smile. "But you do. Because it doesn't matter why you were together. What matters is how you feel. How do you feel?"

"I miss him. Every day. I thought it would get easier. I thought it was just a fluke. But it wasn't."

"Call him." Sam tossed her a phone.

She tossed it back. "I'm not calling him. He hasn't called me. How pathetic would it be to call him? But I would like to see his family. I would like to know how his dad is doing."

"Jesse is great. They put in a couple of stents, changed his medication and he says he hasn't felt this good in years."

"I'm so glad to hear that."

"But you're not going to call. You know, you could call Maria and ask how they're doing. It doesn't have to be about Boone."

"I should call. But who am I to them? No one really." She buried her face in her hands. "I sound pathetic. I'm not a pathetic person."

Samantha tossed a pillow at her. "You're a dork. You're trying to convince yourself that you didn't fall in love with Boone. And while I can't imagine loving him, I get it that he might be appealing to someone else."

"He's amazing."

"Spoken like a woman in love."

"I don't have time for love. I've wasted years of my life. It's time for me to focus on real things. Getting a job. Living a decent life. Going to church with my family. If I toss a relationship into that mix, it's just going to confuse things."

"Or make everything fit together a little better."

"Go away."

"Help me pack boxes. You promised."

Kayla shook her head. "I do not remember making that promise. And he hasn't called me. That should tell me something, right?"

"Yeah, that you're both dorks." Sam headed for the kitchen. "Come on, we'll make a casserole. Potatoes make everything better."

Kayla rode with Sam to Duke's that evening. It was dark when they pulled into town, and obvious that the town was gearing up for the Christmas season. Lights twinkled in the trees along Main Street. Homes and stores were decorated. The nativity had been set up in front of the Community Church.

A few years ago Oregon's dad had slept in that nativity. He'd said if a stable was good enough for his Savior, it was good enough for him.

There was already a crowd at Duke's No Bar and Grill. Kayla strode through the door with Sam. It felt odd to be back, and to know that she belonged here. This was going to be her home. The people waiting at a big table in the center of the dining area were her family. She stopped, taking it in, letting it become real to her.

"You okay?" Sam asked as they walked to that table.

"I'm good."

Remington was there. He stood to hug Kayla and then he reached for Sam, holding her close, their lips brushing lightly.

"Three more days," he whispered.

"And I'll be Samantha Jenkins."

Kayla glanced away because it was too much. She was happy for her sister. But she was feeling sorry for herself. Years ago she'd thought about marriage. She'd dreamed of the man she'd marry, the house they'd live in, even the names of their children. That young girl had dreamed big. There had been mansions and maybe a prince who rescued her.

But then everything had changed. She'd lost her trust. She'd lost track of that innocent girl who dreamed big. She'd been racing through life not allowing herself to think about a future with happily-ever-afters.

"Sit down." Brody pulled on her hand. "And try to relax."

She sat by her brother, and he put a comforting arm around her shoulder.

"I am relaxed." She even managed a smile as she said it.

"Yes, you look relaxed. Do I need to hurt someone for you?"

She shook her head. "No, I'm good. It's just strange, being back. And I'm going to live here. It's a big step."

"You're a country girl at heart. You'll adjust."

Of course she would. She always adjusted. She'd always been good at reinventing herself.

Boone pulled up to Duke's. It had been a couple of weeks since he'd been home so he should have kept on driving. But after playing bodyguard to a Saudi prince for several days, he needed a few minutes to relax. And he needed a piece of Duke's chocolate-cream pie.

As he walked through the door, he realized he should have kept on going. He saw her immediately. She was laughing at something Brody said. But it wasn't her real laugh, not the one that lit up her eyes. It was the laugh that said she was trying hard to fit in.

He wondered if anyone else knew that about her.

Maybe pie wasn't such a great idea. He reached for the door but a hand on his shoulder stopped him. He didn't look up to many people, physically, but he had to look up at Duke Martin.

"Change your mind, Boone?" Duke's hand was still on his shoulder and there was a challenge in his eyes that was unmistakable. "Never figured you for a coward."

"Not a coward, just a man in a hurry to get home. I thought I'd get a piece of pie. To go."

Duke's mouth twisted and his eyes lit with humor. "Sorry, but I don't have pie 'to go.' Pie can only be eaten in house this week."

"Guess I'll come back next week."

"Have a seat, Boone. I wouldn't want you to look yella."

"I'm not yella." Boone headed for a booth. "And the word is *yellow*."

"Yeah, but when you're calling a man *coward*, you say *yella*." Duke grinned. "Sounds better that way."

Boone sat at a booth and took off his hat. He brushed a hand through his hair to smooth it down. He was exhausted. And now he was confused. She was here. He hadn't expected that.

And he hadn't expected the emotional punch to the gut.

Duke sat down across from him, placing the pie on the table just out of reach. Ned, the best waitress in Texas, hurried over to fill his coffee cup. She gave them both a "don't make trouble" look and left.

"You look awful." Duke's hand was on the plate. "As if you really need this pie."

"What I need is for you to stay out of my business."

"But if your business pertains to my family, then it becomes my business."

"Duke, I have to get home. Either give me the pie or don't."

Duke slid the pie in front of him. "What's your hurry? Don't you want to stay and visit? Sam is getting married this weekend. We're having a family dinner. You look as though you could use a good meal."

"I'll have a meal when I get home. And I'm not going to invade your family dinner. I have a family of my own. And from what I hear, a pinkeye outbreak to deal with tomorrow."

"I hear your dad is up and around, doing better now."

"He's doing much better."

Duke sat there, silent, watching him eat the pie. Boone felt about sixteen. He now understood how Remington had felt when the Martins had run him off their ranch a dozen years ago. That had been the first time Rem had tried to date Samantha Martin. It hadn't gone well.

Boone wasn't dating anyone. He definitely wasn't going to start dating clients. When he, Daron and Lucy had started the business, they'd verbally agreed that dating clients was off-limits. It was unprofessional. It created problems.

Big problems. Such as the one he was facing now. He hadn't dated Kayla, but he'd definitely crossed lines. And those lines had led him to this place.

"I have to go."

"Yella."

Boone grabbed his hat and stood. "No, I'm not yella, Duke. I'm a man with a family and a business."

When he walked out the door, he inhaled cool autumn air. It felt good to be back in Texas. He'd spent two weeks in Southern California. It had been hot and dry there. The prince had been a pain. A guy who drove fast and lived faster.

Boone enjoyed the quiet, slow pace of country living. He wouldn't trade Texas for anything. Not even a Bel Air mansion and a Ferrari.

He stood in front of his truck for a long time, staring at Duke's.

Chapter Sixteen

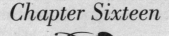

She'd held her breath when he first walked through the door of Duke's. And then she'd held it a little longer while he'd sat at the table with her brother. She'd wanted him to say something. He hadn't. So she'd laughed and talked with her family and pretended it didn't hurt.

It had been an eye-opening experience, though. In the five minutes he'd stayed in the diner she'd realized the truth. She'd been a client to him. Nothing more.

"Ten, nine, eight…" Next to her Brody was counting down.

"What are you doing?" she whispered. Jake was saying something about Sam and Remington and their lives together.

He grinned. "You'll see. Two. One."

Boone pushed open the front door and stepped back inside.

Brody chuckled. "Known him all my life. He can't stand to be called a coward. And he doesn't back down."

Kayla really disliked family at that moment.

"My guess, sis, is you're about to tell us all goodbye."

"I doubt that. I ordered one of Duke's black and bleu steaks, and I plan on eating it."

Boone crossed the diner, and when he reached their table, he looked like a thunderstorm about to break.

"I need for you to come with me," he said to her in a low voice. Everyone was watching, though. Not one person in the suddenly quiet diner had missed the order.

"I'm having dinner with my family." She managed to sound in control. At least she thought so. "And I don't like to be ordered around, Boone."

He briefly closed his eyes. "Can I please have a moment of your time?"

"Now, wasn't that sweet?" Brody said. "I think you should go with him before he tosses you over his shoulder and goes all caveman on us."

Both she and Boone gave Brody a look he

didn't need interpreted for him. Kayla pushed back from the table.

"Five minutes, Boone."

"Ten," he said. He took her hand and led her from the restaurant.

They walked in silence to the park, Boone practically dragging her along with him. Christmas lights twinkled on the trees. A speaker played Christmas music. In the distance she heard a train. Boone still held her hand but his touch had gentled.

"Boone?"

Before she could ask what he wanted he pulled her into his arms.

"Don't talk." His mouth lowered to capture hers in a desperate kiss.

His lips moved over hers and his hands splayed across her back. She didn't feel trapped. She felt complete. For the first time in weeks she didn't wonder. She only wanted. His love. Him.

His lips stilled but his mouth hovered against hers. She felt his smile.

"I missed you." Finally the words she'd longed to hear. "I couldn't drive away from Duke's without holding you, without kissing you. I'm sorry."

"Don't be sorry." She leaned into his shoulder and brushed her lips against his shirt. He smelled so good. Like the mountains and autumn. "I missed you, too."

"How long are you here for?"

"Forever," she answered, her face still buried in the crook of his neck.

"Forever isn't long enough," he told her. "I need more time with you."

"I'm not going anywhere. But what if—"

"No," he said with a voice that shook. "Don't say anything. What I feel has nothing to do with being your bodyguard. It has everything to do with love. I love you, Kayla. And I want more than a few weeks in your life."

She trembled in his arms, thinking about his words. Thinking about forever.

He hadn't planned to put it all out there. He'd gone back into Duke's determined but not knowing where that determination would lead him. He'd only known that he needed to hold her. He had needed to kiss her until the emptiness he'd felt since she'd left went away.

He hadn't expected that one kiss would make him want more. He hadn't planned on any of this, not really.

But she was in his arms, her eyes shining

with emotion that he had to guess meant she felt pretty strongly about him.

And he wanted to marry her. He guessed it was way too early for proposals.

"Say something," he whispered against her hair. "Don't leave me hanging, Stanford."

"Kayla Wilder. I like the way that sounds."

He picked her up and twirled her around him. It wasn't a proposal, but he knew when it was meant to be. He put her back on her own two feet and kissed her again. She wrapped her arms around his neck and held on, as if he was her lifeline.

"I love you, Wilder." She whispered the words a few minutes later. "I'm so glad you're in my life."

"I'm glad to hear that, Stanford. Because I plan on being in your life for a long, long time."

He led her back into Duke's, back to her family. But this time he stayed. He let the Martin brothers tease him. He endured the looks from the women.

Kayla sitting next to him was all that mattered.

Epilogue

Kayla walked out of the school on a sunny day at the end of May. She'd been a substitute teacher since December. Last week the school had offered her a permanent position as a second-grade teacher.

She had found herself in Martin's Crossing. She had a career she loved. She had a home, the cottage Samantha had vacated. Duke had given her a pretty bay gelding.

She had a man who cherished her. And she loved him right back. He had texted her an hour earlier asking her to meet him after school. He wanted to take her on a date.

He was waiting in the parking lot. Gorgeous. He was absolutely gorgeous. Even from a distance she knew she could drown in his espresso eyes. He had a dimple in his right cheek that she enjoyed kissing.

He smelled like mountains and autumn air. And in jeans low on his hips and a T-shirt that hugged his shoulders, no one was more gorgeous.

"You coming with me, Stanford?" he called out from the tractor he'd driven to town to pick her up in.

"I'm coming, Wilder." She crossed the parking lot as he got down from the tractor to open the door for her. "My chariot awaits. This is going to be some date."

"Honey, we do things right here in the country." He winked as he said it and he climbed up in the seat with her. "Do not touch anything."

"I wouldn't dream of it." So she scooted to the far side of the tractor.

Then he kissed her. "I've been waiting two days for that. You aren't going to deny me."

"I wouldn't dream of it."

They drove out to the Wilder ranch, cars passing them one at a time. He pulled onto the drive and through a gate. She remembered this field. They'd been here before. Last fall when he hadn't cut down the wildflowers.

"I brought a picnic from Duke's." He pointed to the bag of carryout food on the floor.

"Sounds perfect."

The tractor chugged along over rolling

hills. When it got to that same back pasture, he stopped. Bluebonnets spread out before them, making a carpet of wildflowers.

"Isn't this something?" he asked. "They've been blooming for a while. I should have brought you sooner."

"No, this is perfect."

They climbed down from the tractor and he led her through the field of flowers and down to the creek.

"There's nowhere else like it."

"No, there isn't." She turned to look at the field behind them, captured in late-afternoon sunlight. The bluebonnets stretched to the base of the distant hill.

"I'd like to build our house here," he said. The words hung in the air, like the sweet scent of wildflowers.

"*Our* house?" She looked up at him, sensing the moment, her heart skipping along in agreement.

"Yes, *our* house." He spoke as if he was talking about the weather. She wanted to hit him.

"When would we build this house?" She tried to match his tone of indifference.

"We could start in a month or so and have it finished and ready to move into this fall."

"This fall? But aren't you forgetting something?" she asked, as serious as she could be when she saw the teasing glint in his eyes.

"Have I forgotten something?"

She nodded, her breath catching as he reached for her.

His hand brushed down her arm and he took her hand in his. And then he went down on one knee and smiled up at her, that mischievous light in his dark eyes turning to something warmer and undoing her composure.

"Kayla Stanford, will you marry me? And live here in this field of bluebonnets? We could build a big house and fill it with pretty little girls and ornery boys. If you'll just say yes."

He pulled a ring from his pocket and held it up, waiting.

"Yes. Oh, Boone, yes." She pulled him to his feet and he slid the ring on her finger. "I want to marry you. I want to have a farmhouse and babies. With you."

He kissed her then, and she sank into his embrace. She was home. And she couldn't imagine being anywhere but in his arms.

* * * * *

Dear Reader,

It is so hard to believe we've been in Martin's Crossing for over a year! Kayla Stanford, heroine in *Her Rancher Bodyguard*, is a half sibling to the Martins. She's a little lost but a whole lot determined. Her journey to Martin's Crossing and into the life of Boone Wilder and his family will help her discover her softer side. She'll find that there are people she can trust, with her life and her heart.

I hope you enjoy this addition to the Martin's Crossing series!

Brenda

LARGER-PRINT BOOKS!

GET 2 FREE LARGER-PRINT NOVELS PLUS 2 FREE MYSTERY GIFTS

Love Inspired®

SUSPENSE
RIVETING INSPIRATIONAL ROMANCE

Larger-print novels are now available...

READERSERVICE.COM

Manage your account online!

- Review your order history
- Manage your payments
- Update your address

> ### *We've designed the Reader Service website just for you.*

Enjoy all the features!

- Discover new series available to you, and read excerpts from any series.
- Respond to mailings and special monthly offers.
- Connect with favorite authors at the blog.
- Browse the Bonus Bucks catalog and online-only exculsives.
- Share your feedback.

Visit us at:
ReaderService.com

RS15

LARGER-PRINT BOOKS!

GET 2 FREE
LARGER-PRINT NOVELS
PLUS 2 FREE
MYSTERY GIFTS

Love Inspired®

Larger-print novels are now available...

LILP15